THE GL
BARTON PEVERIL ᴗ
Renew via *bit.do/glynlibraryrenew* ᵥ
This item must be retur

PULP

PULP, January 2021.

First printing. Published by Image Comics, Inc. Office of publication: PO BOX 14457, Portland, OR 97293.

 Publication design by Sean Phillips

by Ed Brubaker and Sean Phillips

L P

Colors by Jacob Phillips

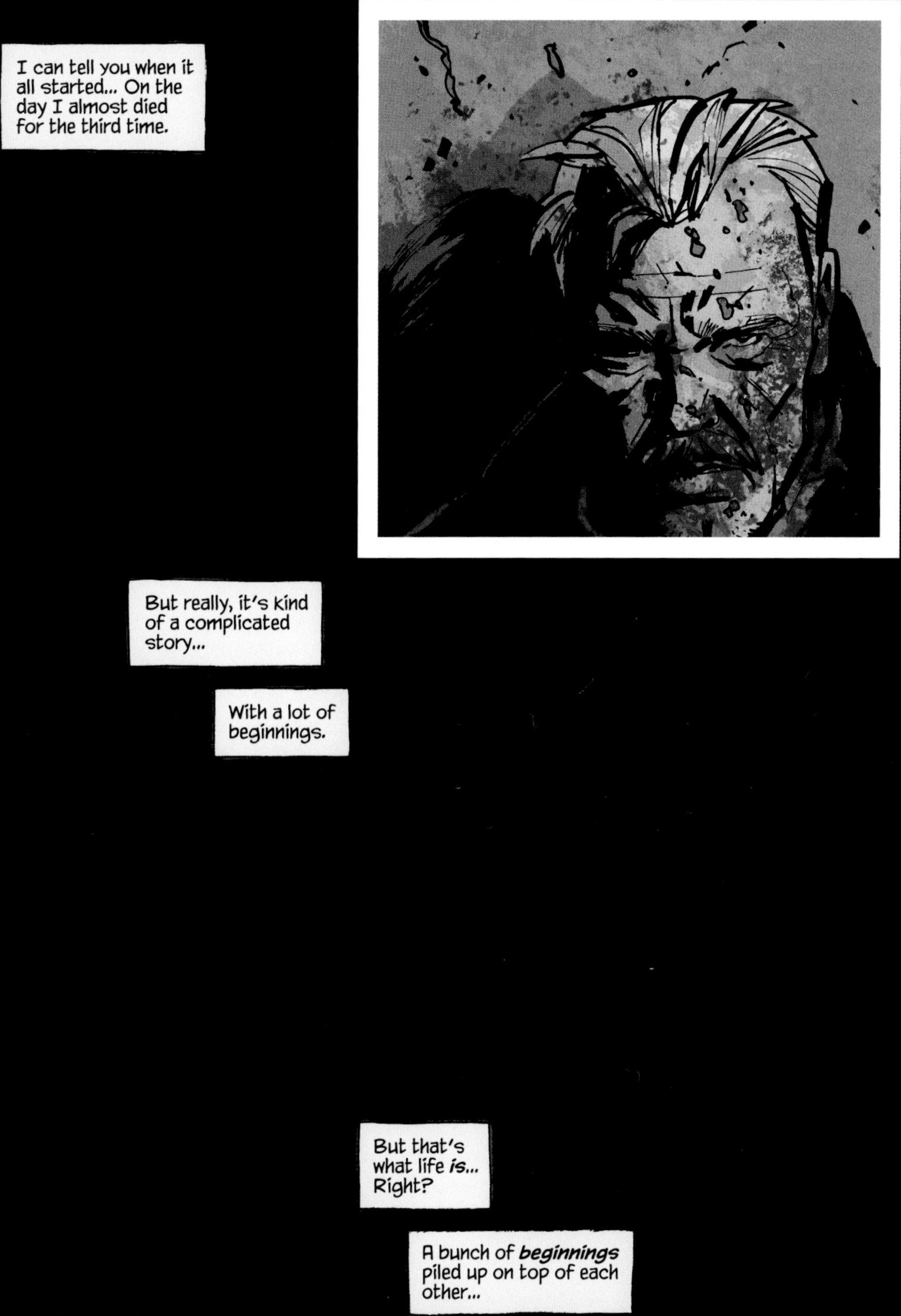
I can tell you when it all started... On the day I almost died for the third time.
But really, it's kind of a complicated story...
With a lot of beginnings.
But that's what life *is*... Right?
A bunch of ***beginnings*** piled up on top of each other...

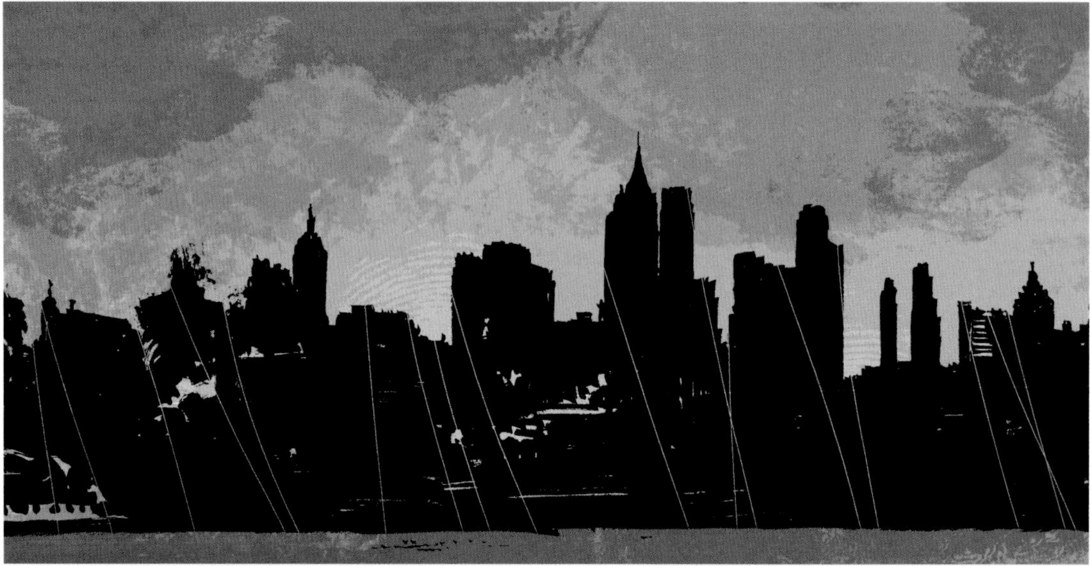

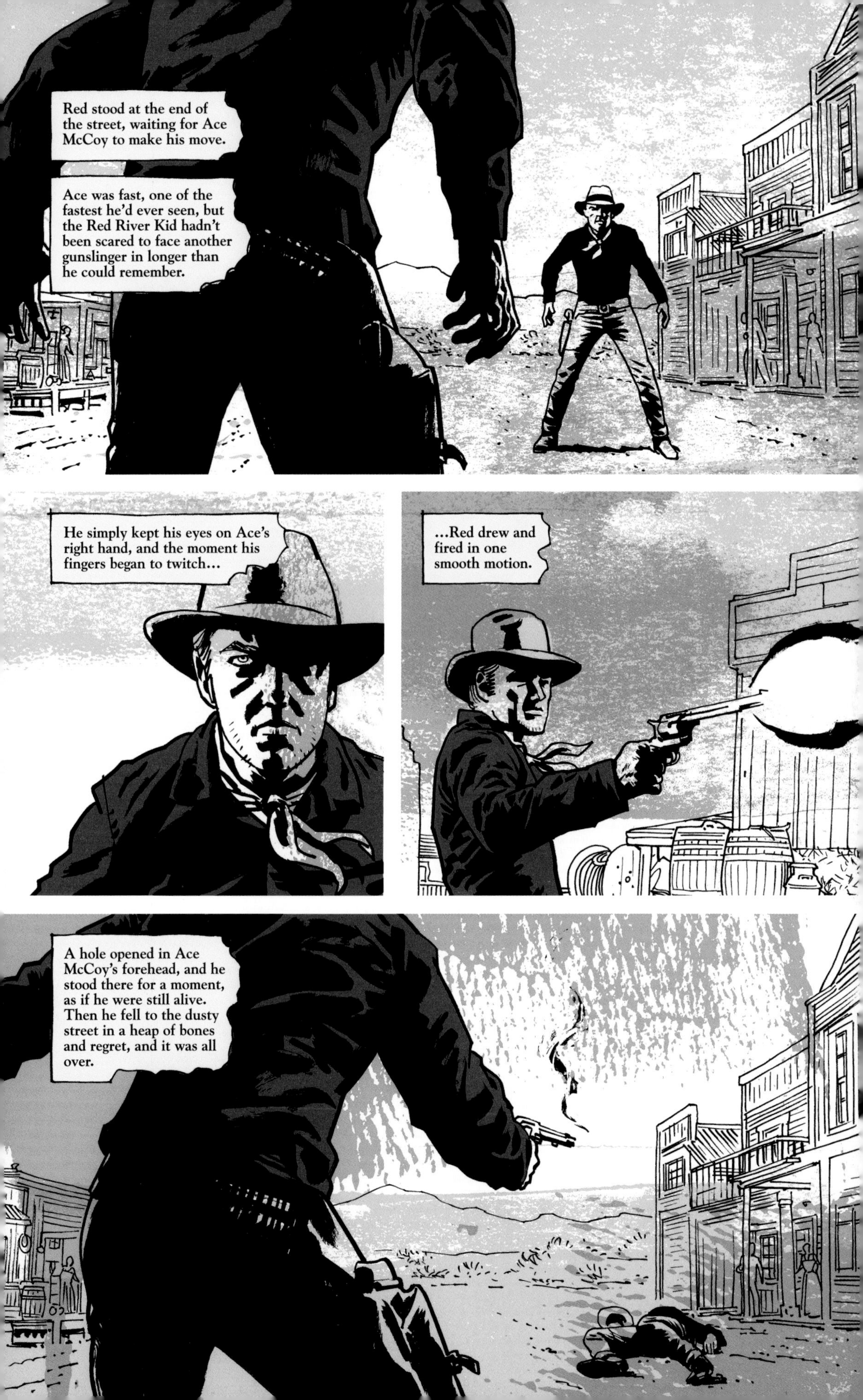
Red stood at the end of the street, waiting for Ace McCoy to make his move.
Ace was fast, one of the fastest he'd ever seen, but the Red River Kid hadn't been scared to face another gunslinger in longer than he could remember.
He simply kept his eyes on Ace's right hand, and the moment his fingers began to twitch...
...Red drew and fired in one smooth motion.
A hole opened in Ace McCoy's forehead, and he stood there for a moment, as if he were still alive. Then he fell to the dusty street in a heap of bones and regret, and it was all over.

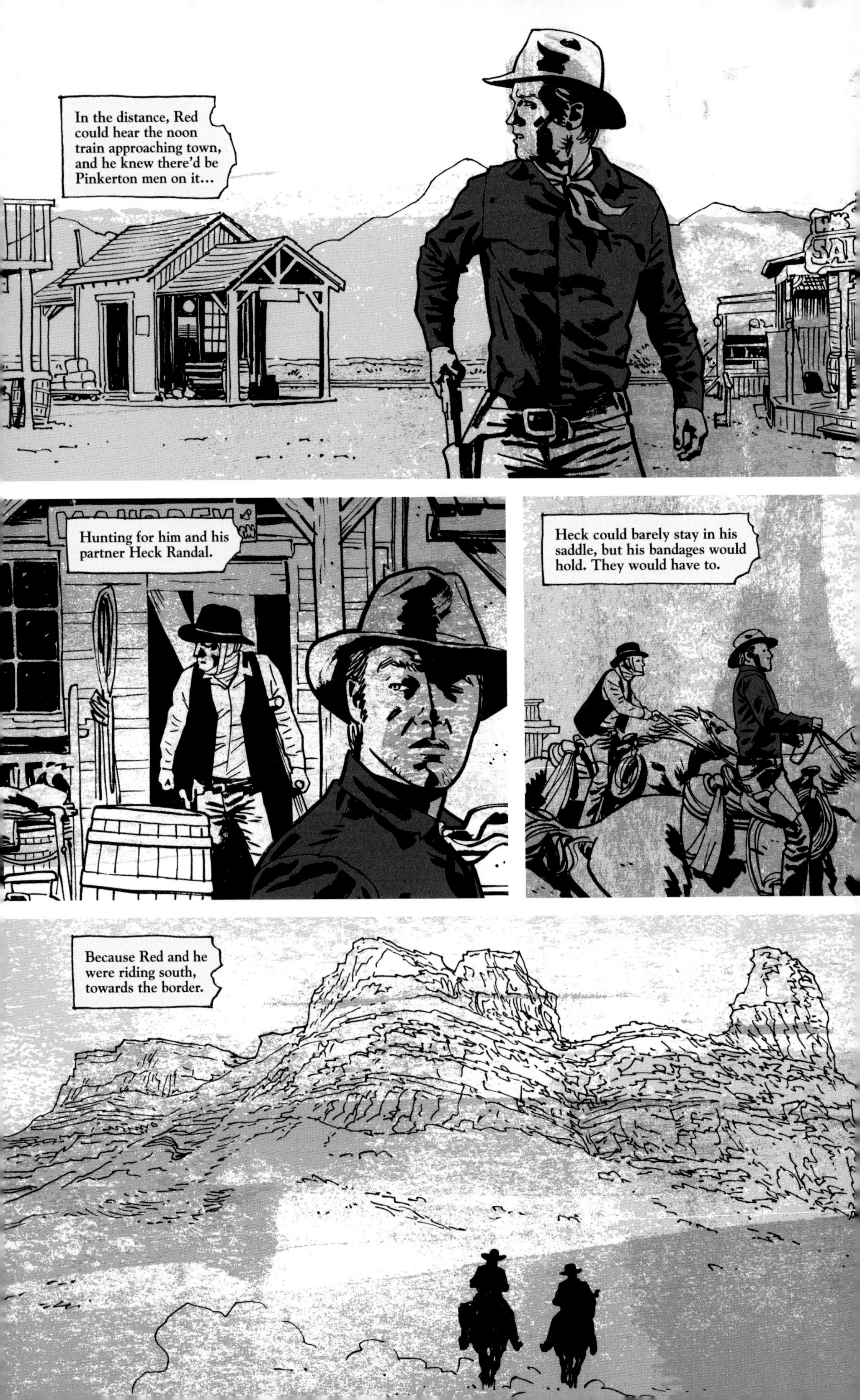
In the distance, Red could hear the noon train approaching town, and he knew there'd be Pinkerton men on it...
Hunting for him and his partner Heck Randal.
Heck could barely stay in his saddle, but his bandages would hold. They would have to.
Because Red and he were riding south, towards the border.

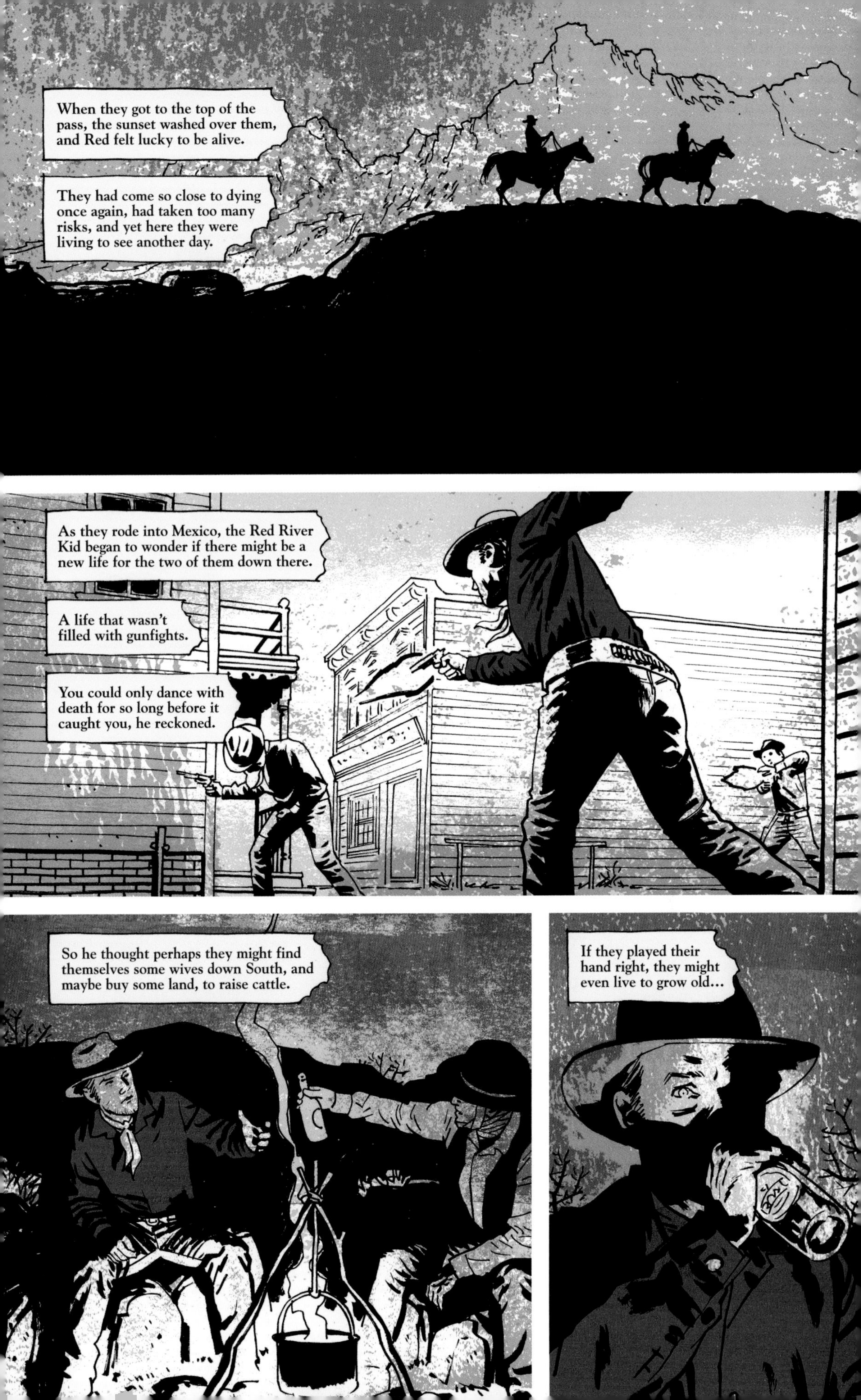
When they got to the top of the pass, the sunset washed over them, and Red felt lucky to be alive.
They had come so close to dying once again, had taken too many risks, and yet here they were living to see another day.
As they rode into Mexico, the Red River Kid began to wonder if there might be a new life for the two of them down there.
A life that wasn't filled with gunfights.
You could only dance with death for so long before it caught you, he reckoned.
So he thought perhaps they might find themselves some wives down South, and maybe buy some land, to raise cattle.
If they played their hand right, they might even live to grow old...

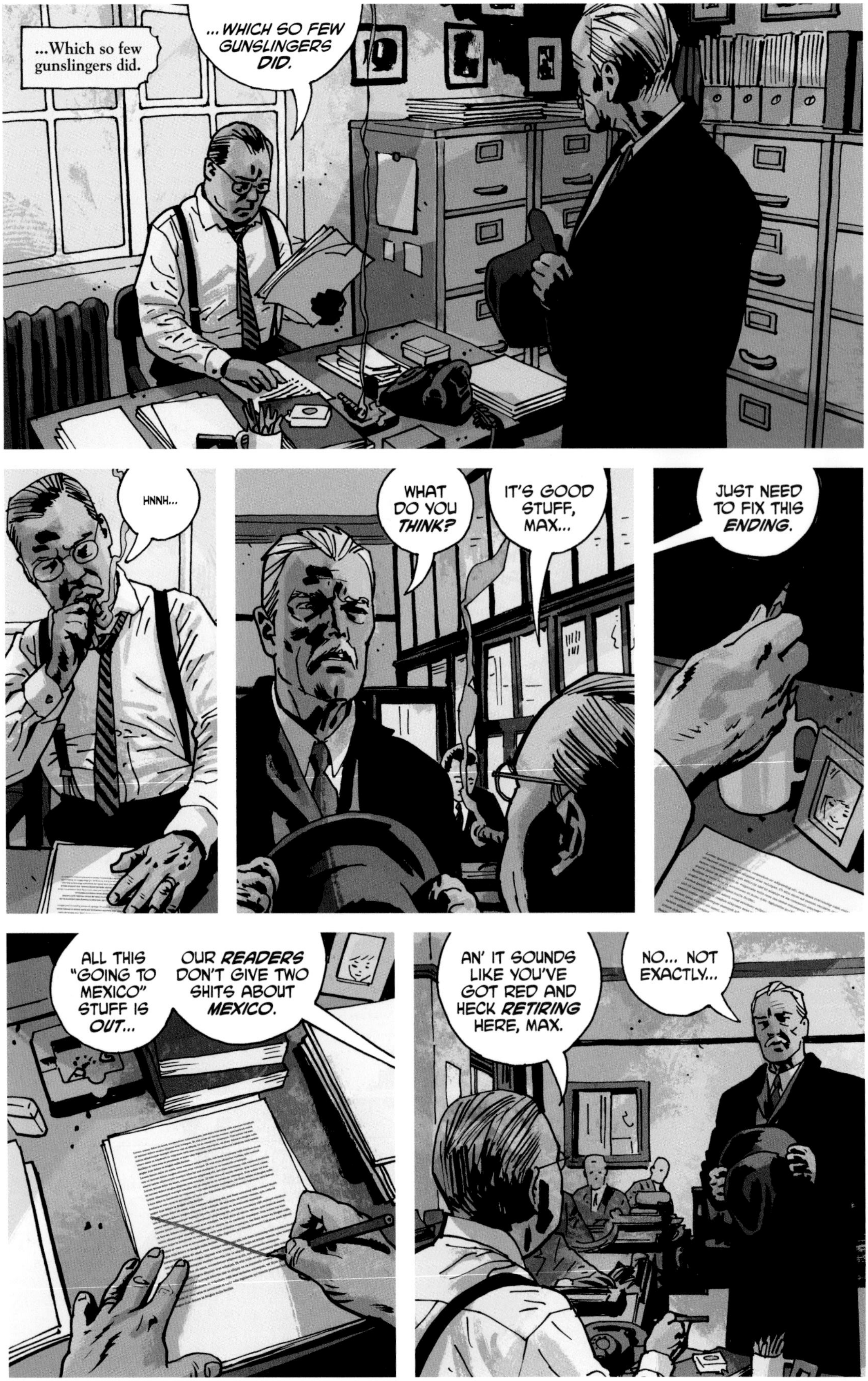
...Which so few gunslingers did.
...WHICH SO FEW GUNSLINGERS DID.
HNNH...
WHAT DO YOU THINK?
IT'S GOOD STUFF, MAX...
JUST NEED TO FIX THIS ENDING.
ALL THIS "GOING TO MEXICO" STUFF IS OUT...
OUR READERS DON'T GIVE TWO SHITS ABOUT MEXICO.
AN' IT SOUNDS LIKE YOU'VE GOT RED AND HECK RETIRING HERE, MAX.
NO... NOT EXACTLY...

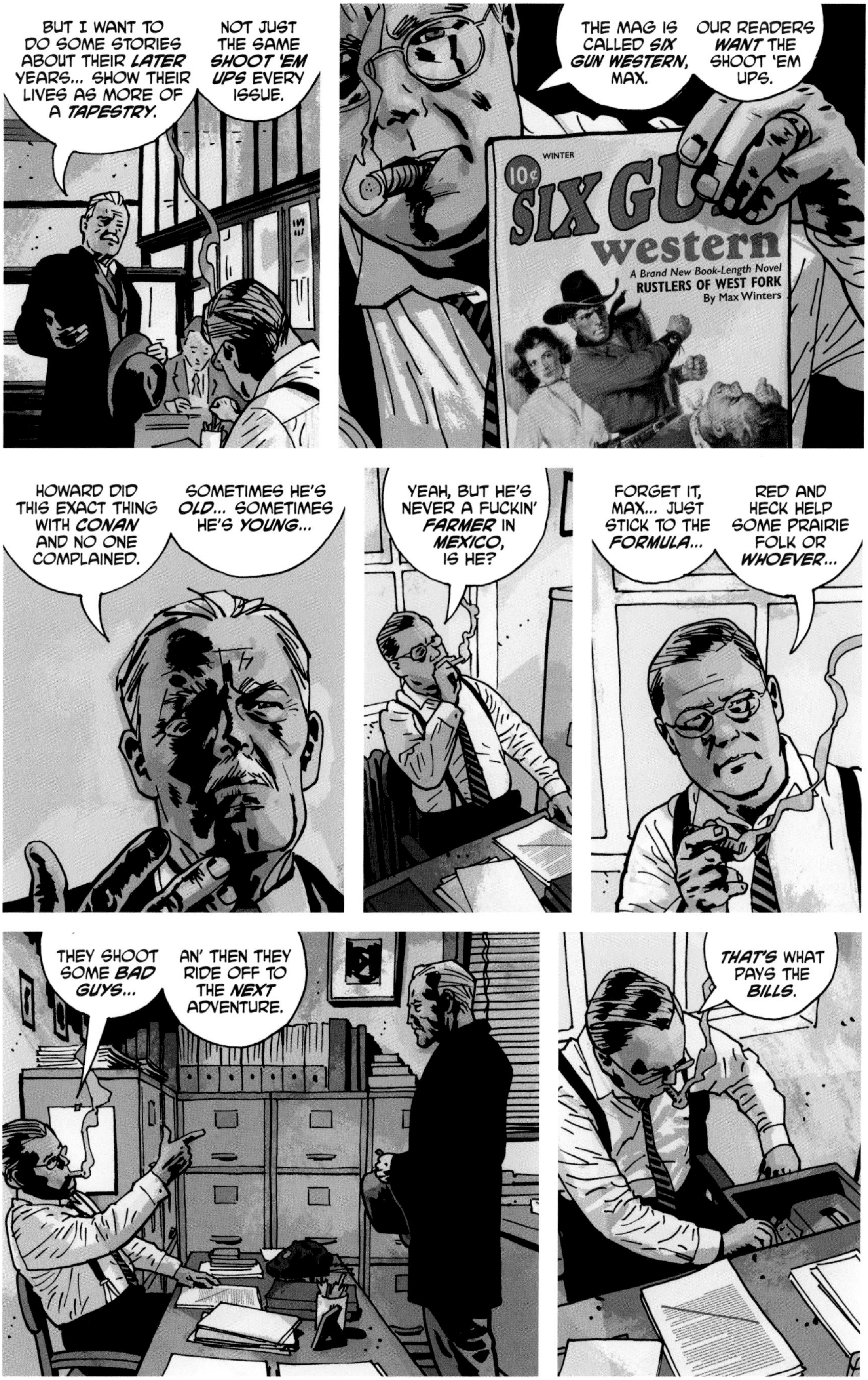
BUT I WANT TO DO SOME STORIES ABOUT THEIR LATER YEARS... SHOW THEIR LIVES AS MORE OF A TAPESTRY.
NOT JUST THE SAME SHOOT 'EM UPS EVERY ISSUE.
THE MAG IS CALLED SIX GUN WESTERN, MAX.
OUR READERS WANT THE SHOOT 'EM UPS.
WINTER
10¢
SIX GU
western
A Brand New Book-Length Novel
RUSTLERS OF WEST FORK
By Max Winters
HOWARD DID THIS EXACT THING WITH CONAN AND NO ONE COMPLAINED.
SOMETIMES HE'S OLD... SOMETIMES HE'S YOUNG...
YEAH, BUT HE'S NEVER A FUCKIN' FARMER IN MEXICO, IS HE?
FORGET IT, MAX... JUST STICK TO THE FORMULA...
RED AND HECK HELP SOME PRAIRIE FOLK OR WHOEVER...
THEY SHOOT SOME BAD GUYS...
AN' THEN THEY RIDE OFF TO THE NEXT ADVENTURE.
THAT'S WHAT PAYS THE BILLS.

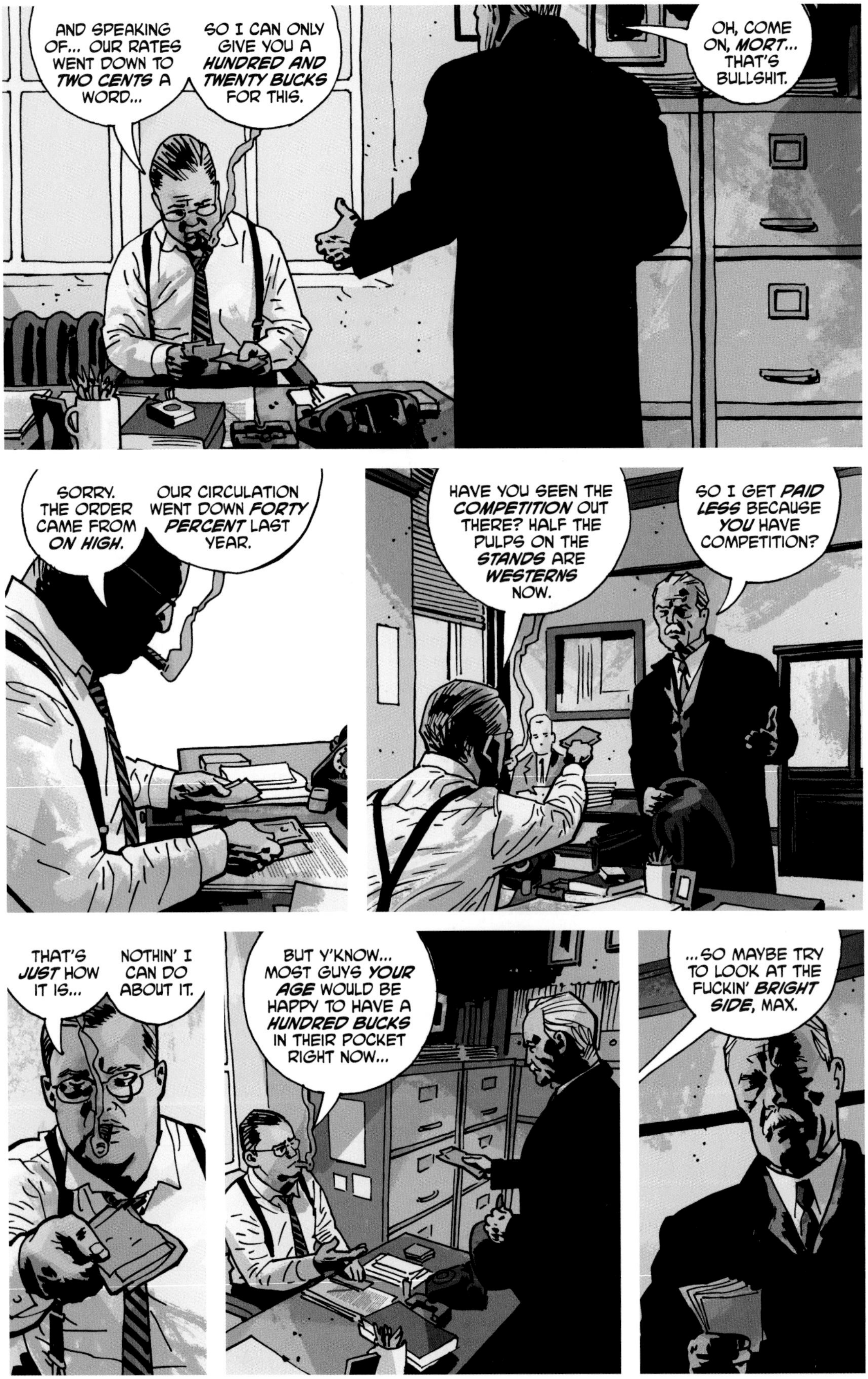
AND SPEAKING OF... OUR RATES WENT DOWN TO *TWO CENTS* A WORD...
SO I CAN ONLY GIVE YOU A *HUNDRED AND TWENTY BUCKS* FOR THIS.
OH, COME ON, *MORT*... THAT'S BULLSHIT.
SORRY. THE ORDER CAME FROM *ON HIGH*.
OUR CIRCULATION WENT DOWN *FORTY PERCENT* LAST YEAR.
HAVE YOU SEEN THE *COMPETITION* OUT THERE? HALF THE PULPS ON THE *STANDS* ARE *WESTERNS* NOW.
SO I GET *PAID LESS* BECAUSE *YOU* HAVE COMPETITION?
THAT'S *JUST* HOW IT IS...
NOTHIN' I CAN DO ABOUT IT.
BUT Y'KNOW... MOST GUYS *YOUR AGE* WOULD BE HAPPY TO HAVE A *HUNDRED BUCKS* IN THEIR POCKET RIGHT NOW...
...SO MAYBE TRY TO LOOK AT THE FUCKIN' *BRIGHT SIDE*, MAX.

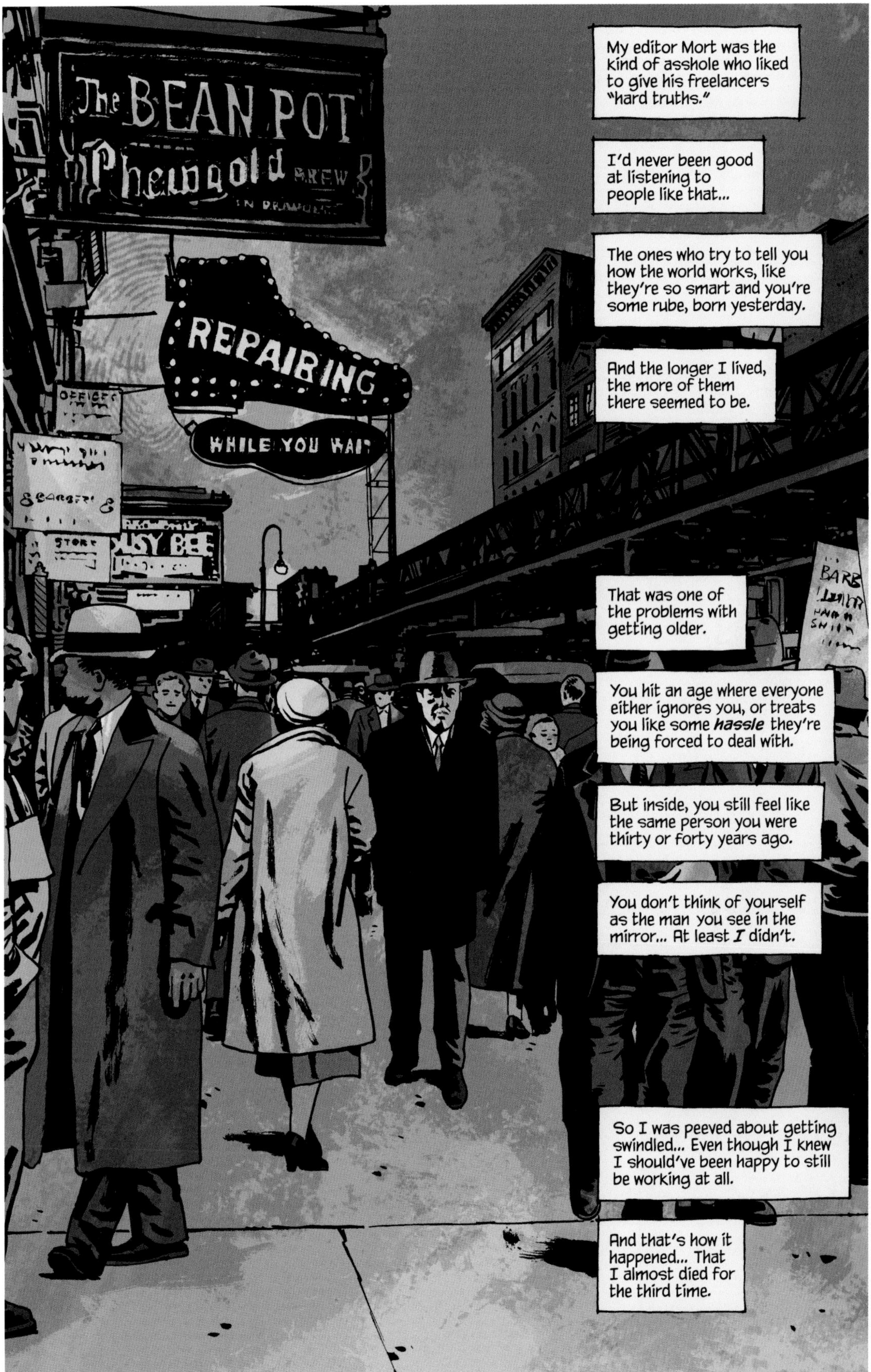
The BEAN POT
Rheingold BREW
REPAIRING
WHILE YOU WAIT
My editor Mort was the kind of asshole who liked to give his freelancers "hard truths."
I'd never been good at listening to people like that...
The ones who try to tell you how the world works, like they're so smart and you're some rube, born yesterday.
And the longer I lived, the more of them there seemed to be.
That was one of the problems with getting older.
You hit an age where everyone either ignores you, or treats you like some *hassle* they're being forced to deal with.
But inside, you still feel like the same person you were thirty or forty years ago.
You don't think of yourself as the man you see in the mirror... At least *I* didn't.
So I was peeved about getting swindled... Even though I knew I should've been happy to still be working at all.
And that's how it happened... That I almost died for the third time.

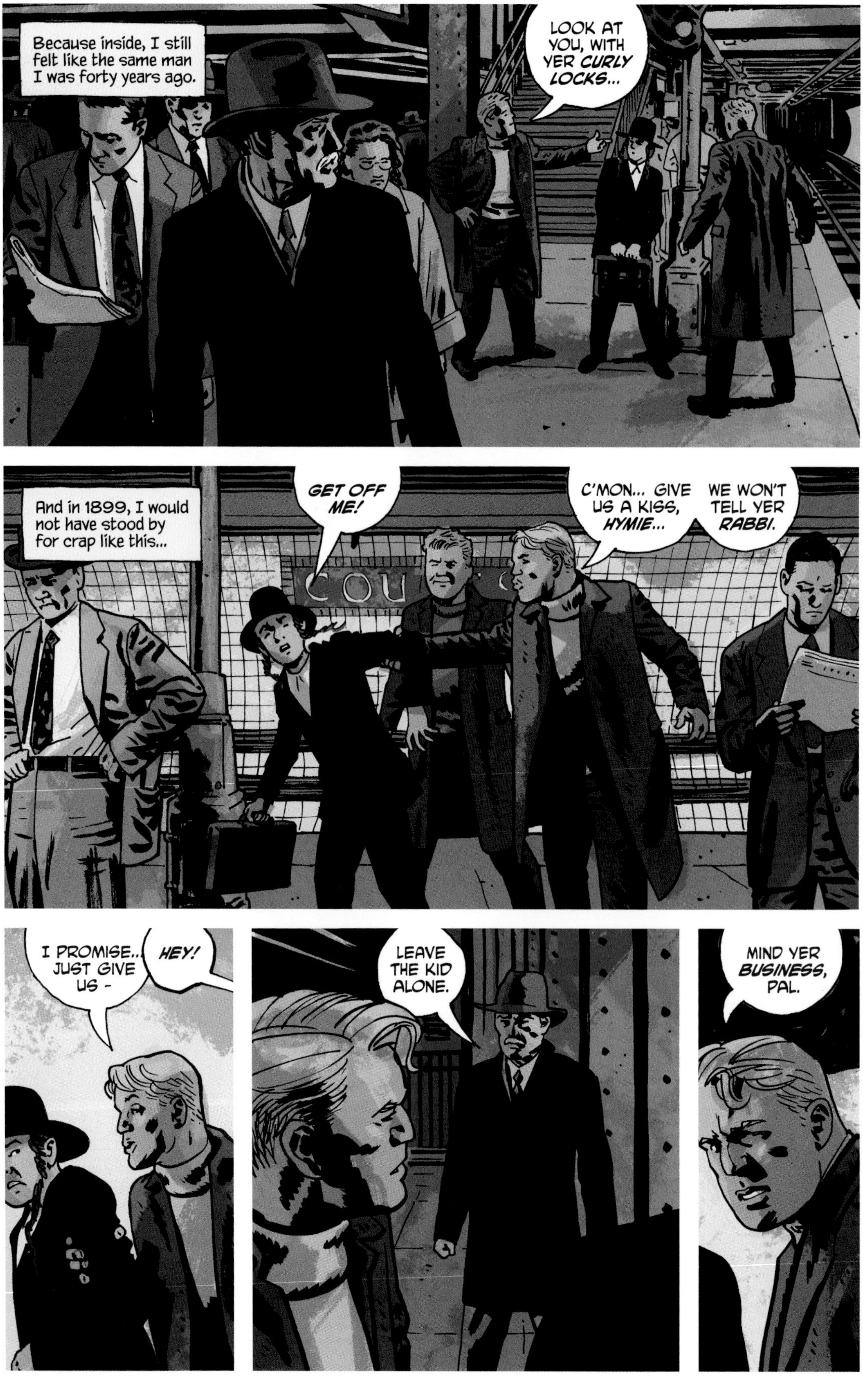
Because inside, I still felt like the same man I was forty years ago.
LOOK AT YOU, WITH YER CURLY LOCKS...
And in 1899, I would not have stood by for crap like this...
GET OFF ME!
C'MON... GIVE US A KISS, HYMIE...
WE WON'T TELL YER RABBI.
COU
I PROMISE... JUST GIVE US -
HEY!
LEAVE THE KID ALONE.
MIND YER BUSINESS, PAL.

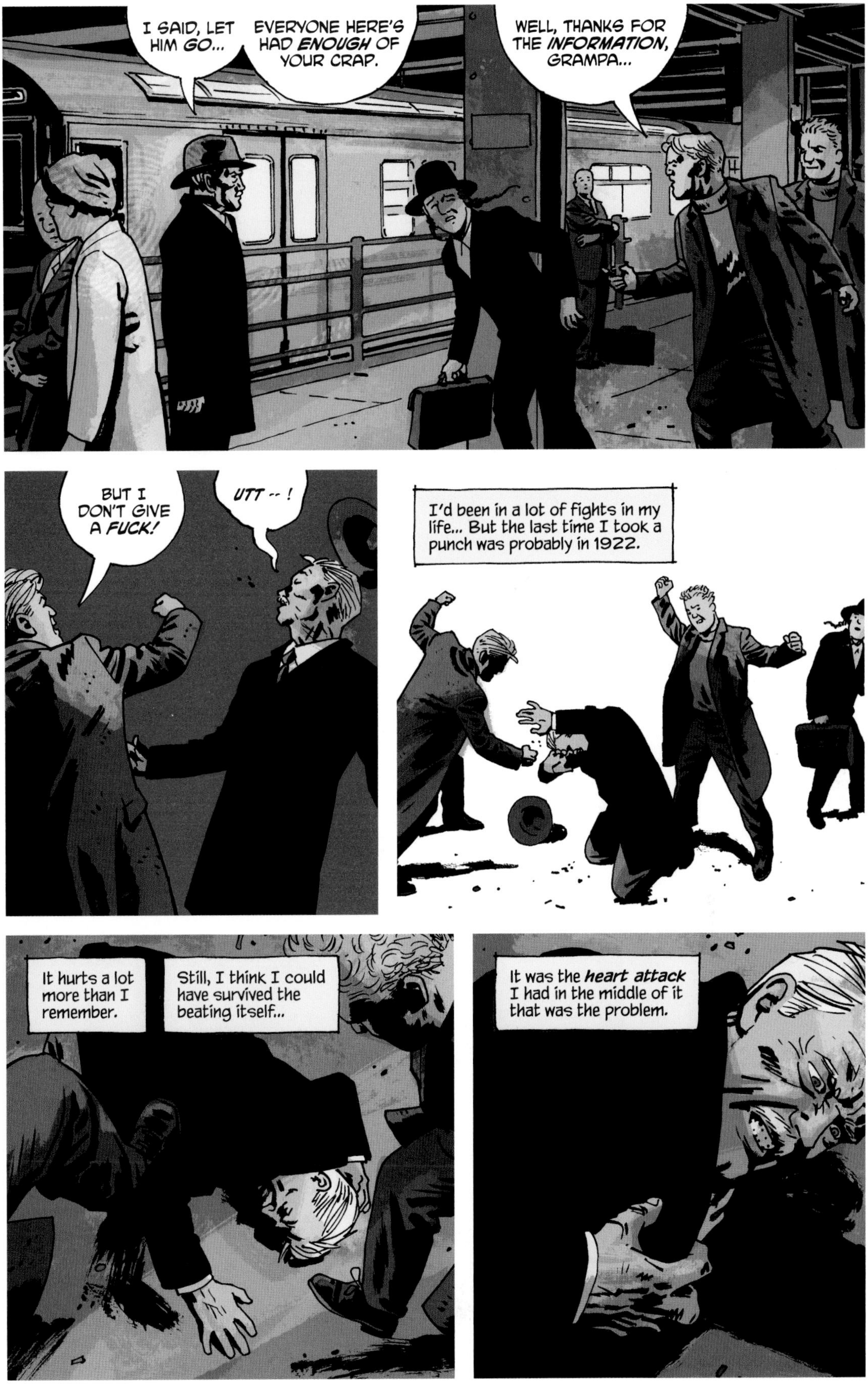

I SAID, LET HIM GO...
EVERYONE HERE'S HAD ENOUGH OF YOUR CRAP.
WELL, THANKS FOR THE INFORMATION, GRAMPA...
BUT I DON'T GIVE A FUCK!
UTT -- !
I'd been in a lot of fights in my life... But the last time I took a punch was probably in 1922.
It hurts a lot more than I remember.
Still, I think I could have survived the beating itself...
It was the heart attack I had in the middle of it that was the problem.

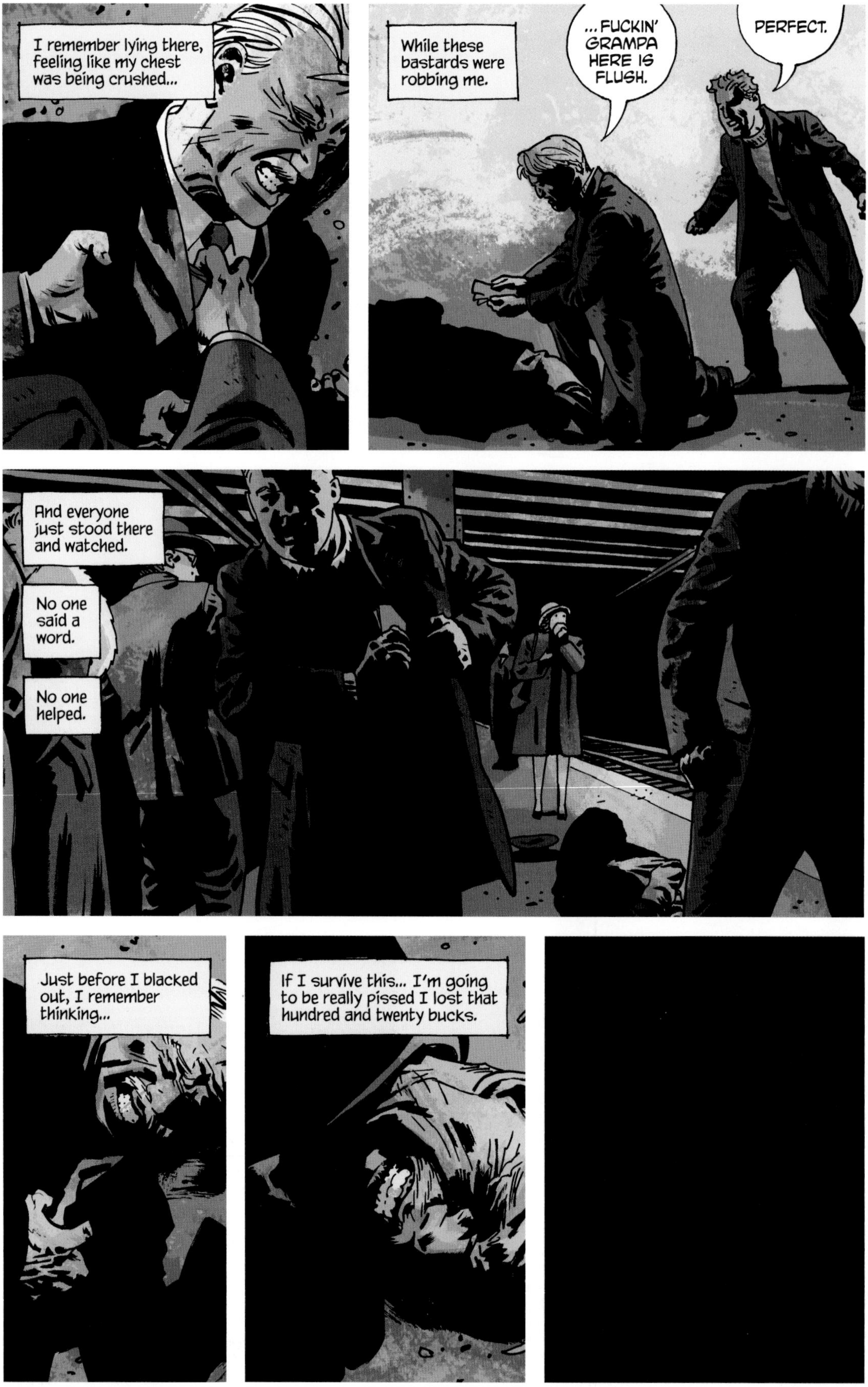
I remember lying there, feeling like my chest was being crushed...
While these bastards were robbing me.
...FUCKIN' GRAMPA HERE IS FLUSH.
PERFECT.
And everyone just stood there and watched.
No one said a word.
No one helped.
Just before I blacked out, I remember thinking...
If I survive this... I'm going to be really pissed I lost that hundred and twenty bucks.

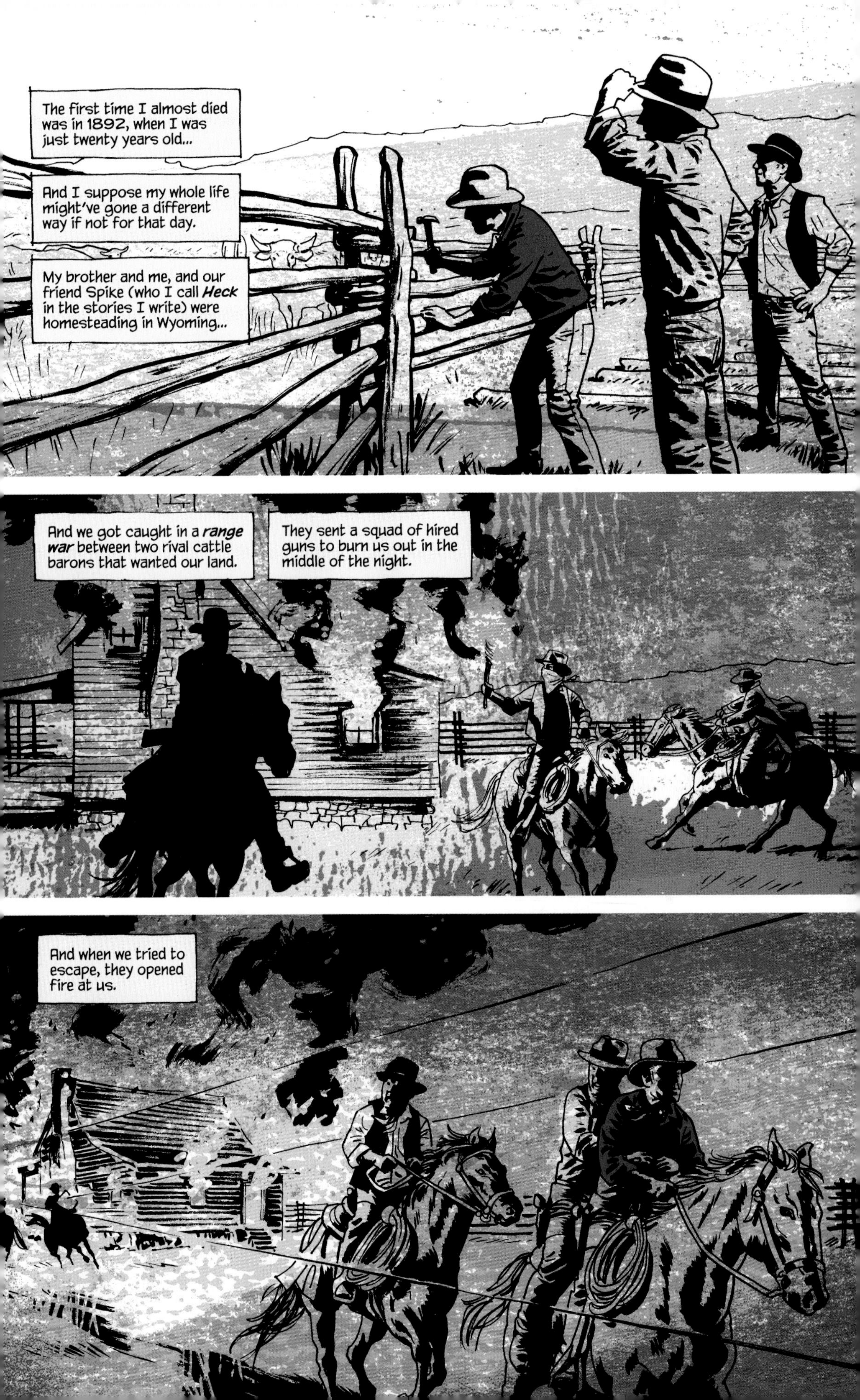
The first time I almost died was in 1892, when I was just twenty years old...
And I suppose my whole life might've gone a different way if not for that day.
My brother and me, and our friend Spike (who I call *Heck* in the stories I write) were homesteading in Wyoming...
And we got caught in a *range war* between two rival cattle barons that wanted our land.
They sent a squad of hired guns to burn us out in the middle of the night.
And when we tried to escape, they opened fire at us.

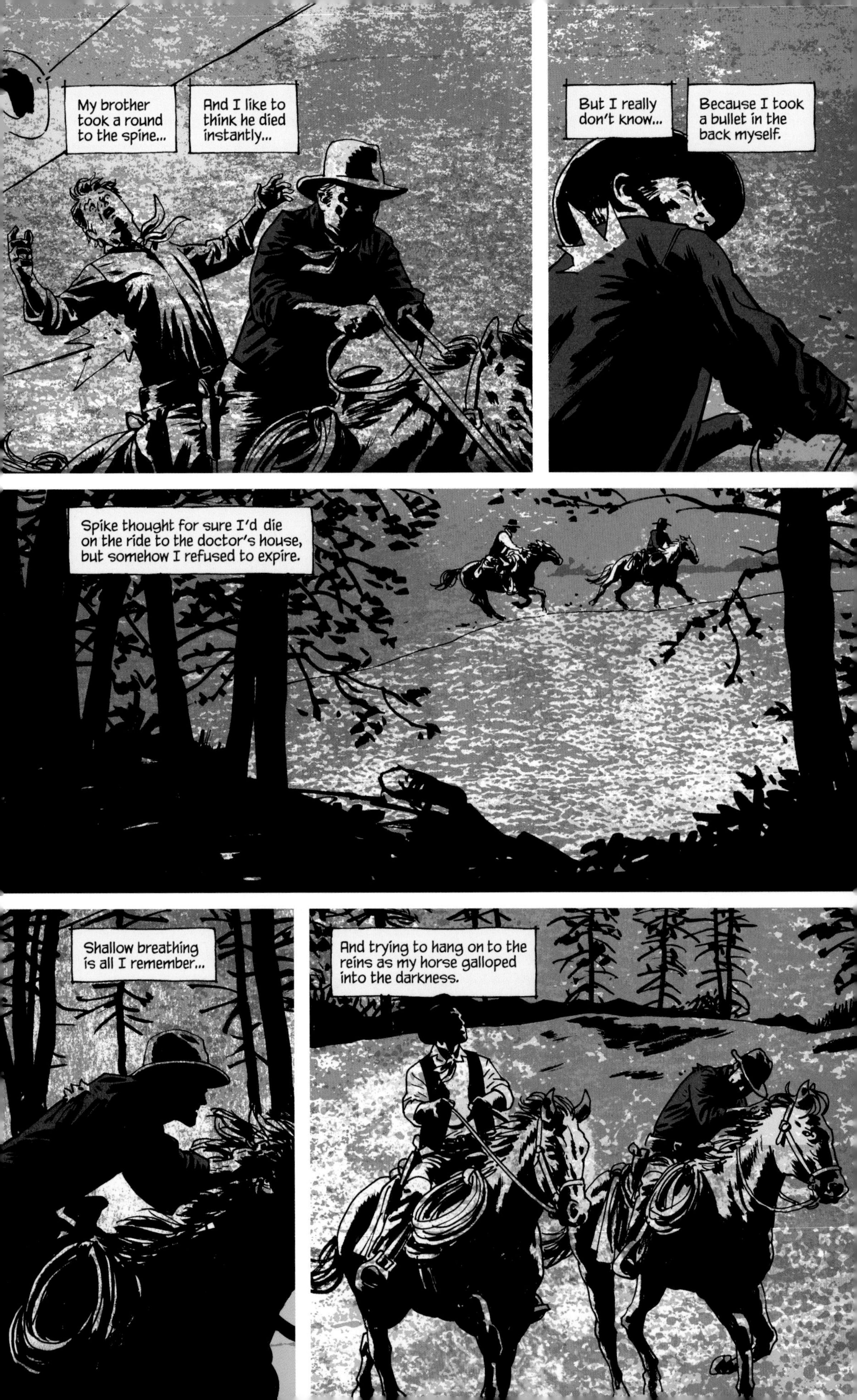
My brother took a round to the spine...
And I like to think he died instantly...
But I really don't know...
Because I took a bullet in the back myself.
Spike thought for sure I'd die on the ride to the doctor's house, but somehow I refused to expire.
Shallow breathing is all I remember...
And trying to hang on to the reins as my horse galloped into the darkness.

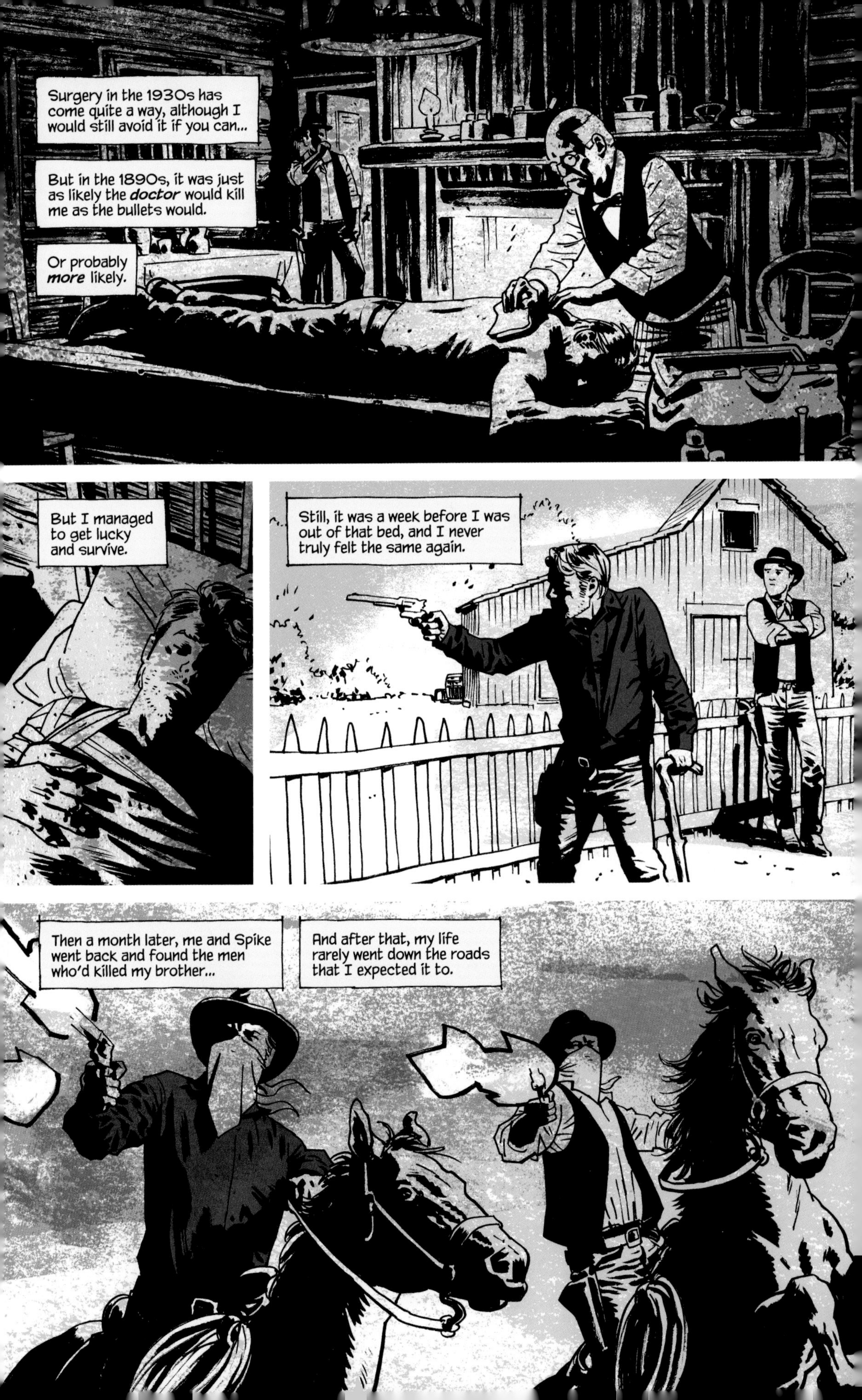
Surgery in the 1930s has come quite a way, although I would still avoid it if you can...
But in the 1890s, it was just as likely the *doctor* would kill me as the bullets would.
Or probably *more* likely.
But I managed to get lucky and survive.
Still, it was a week before I was out of that bed, and I never truly felt the same again.
Then a month later, me and Spike went back and found the men who'd killed my brother...
And after that, my life rarely went down the roads that I expected it to.

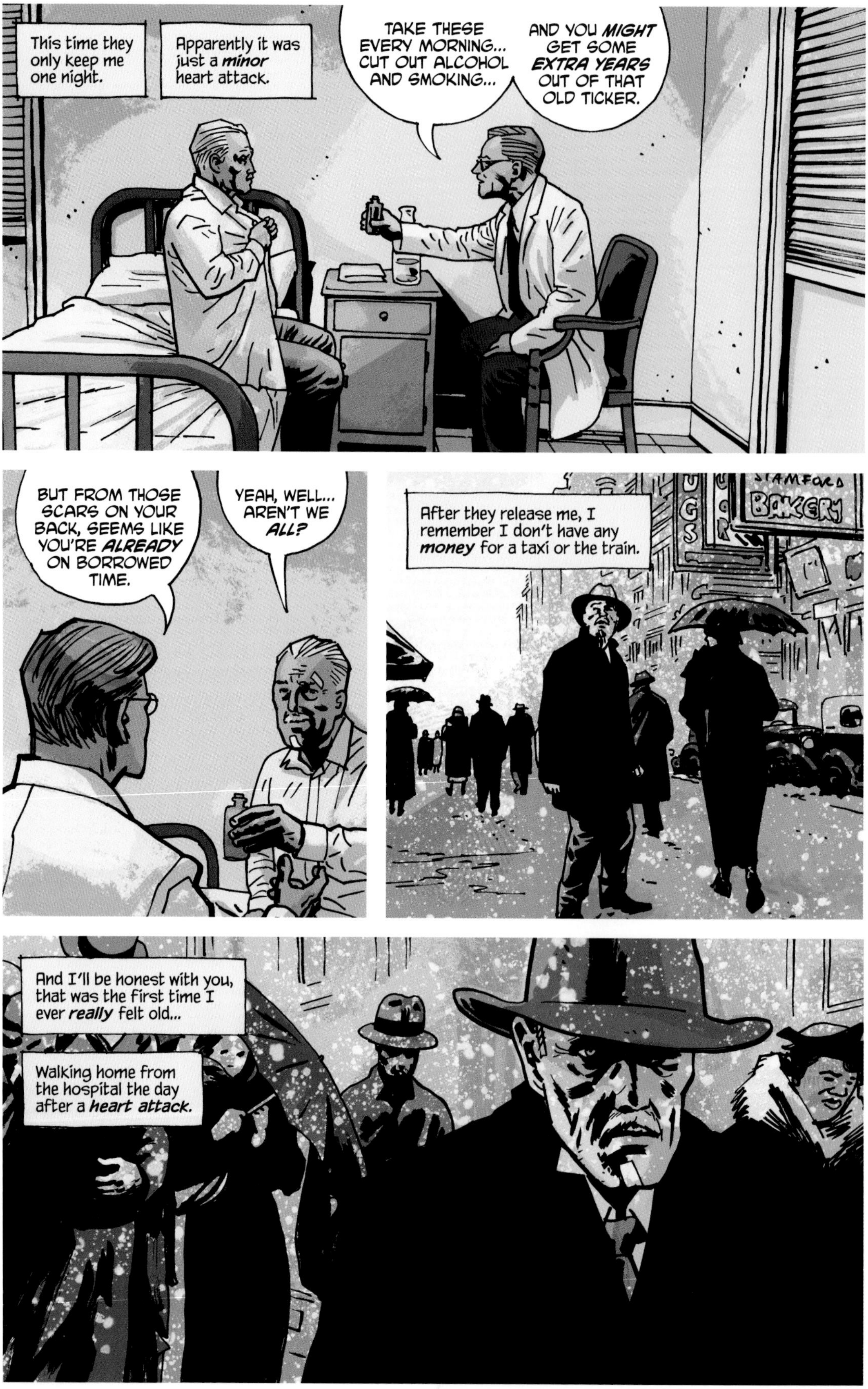

This time they only keep me one night.
Apparently it was just a *minor* heart attack.
TAKE THESE EVERY MORNING... CUT OUT ALCOHOL AND SMOKING...
AND YOU *MIGHT* GET SOME *EXTRA YEARS* OUT OF THAT OLD TICKER.
BUT FROM THOSE SCARS ON YOUR BACK, SEEMS LIKE YOU'RE *ALREADY* ON BORROWED TIME.
YEAH, WELL... AREN'T WE *ALL?*
After they release me, I remember I don't have any *money* for a taxi or the train.
STAMFORD
BAKERY
And I'll be honest with you, that was the first time I ever *really* felt old...
Walking home from the hospital the day after a *heart attack.*

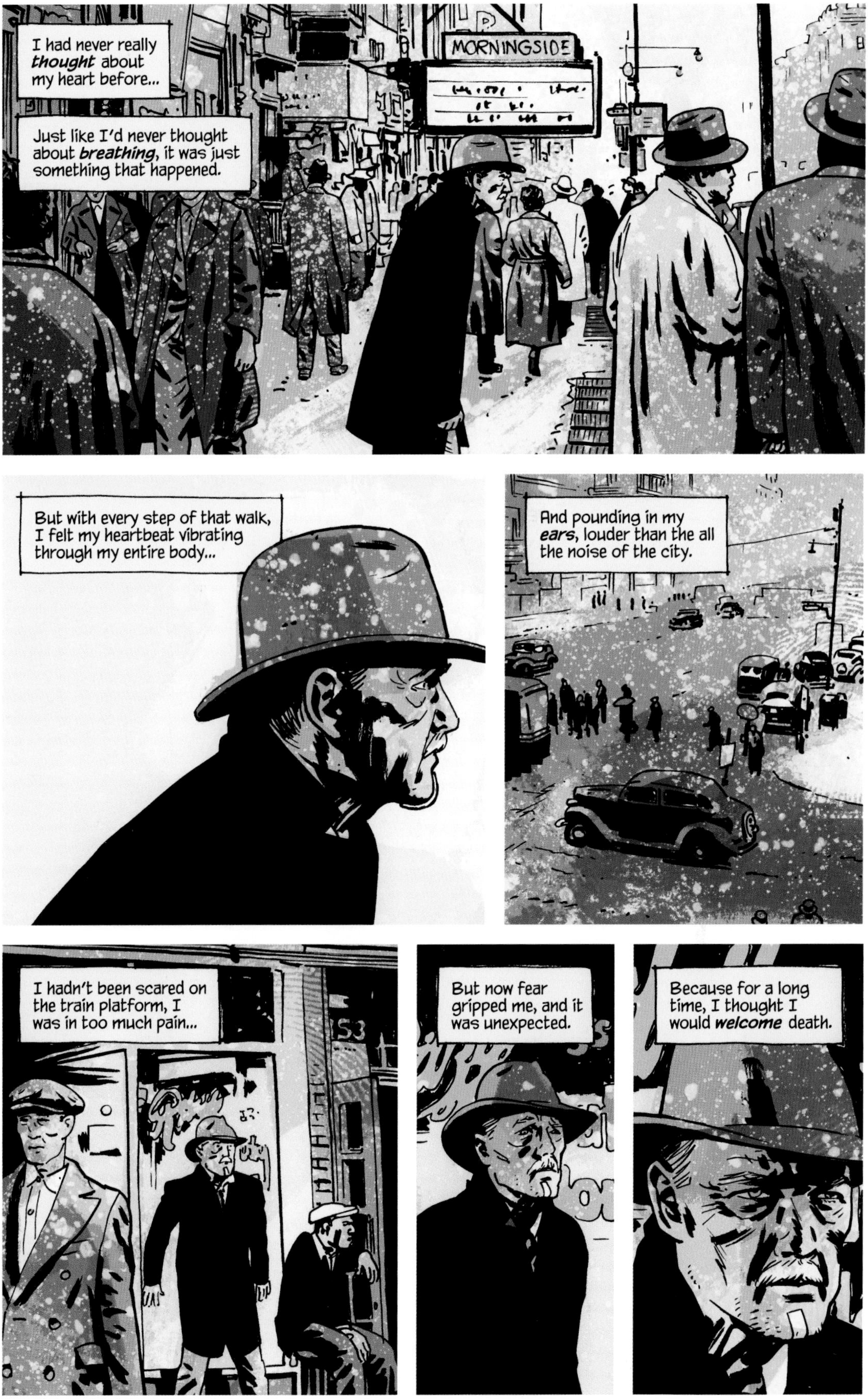
MORNINGSIDE
I had never really thought about my heart before...
Just like I'd never thought about breathing, it was just something that happened.
But with every step of that walk, I felt my heartbeat vibrating through my entire body...
And pounding in my ears, louder than the all the noise of the city.
I hadn't been scared on the train platform, I was in too much pain...
But now fear gripped me, and it was unexpected.
Because for a long time, I thought I would welcome death.

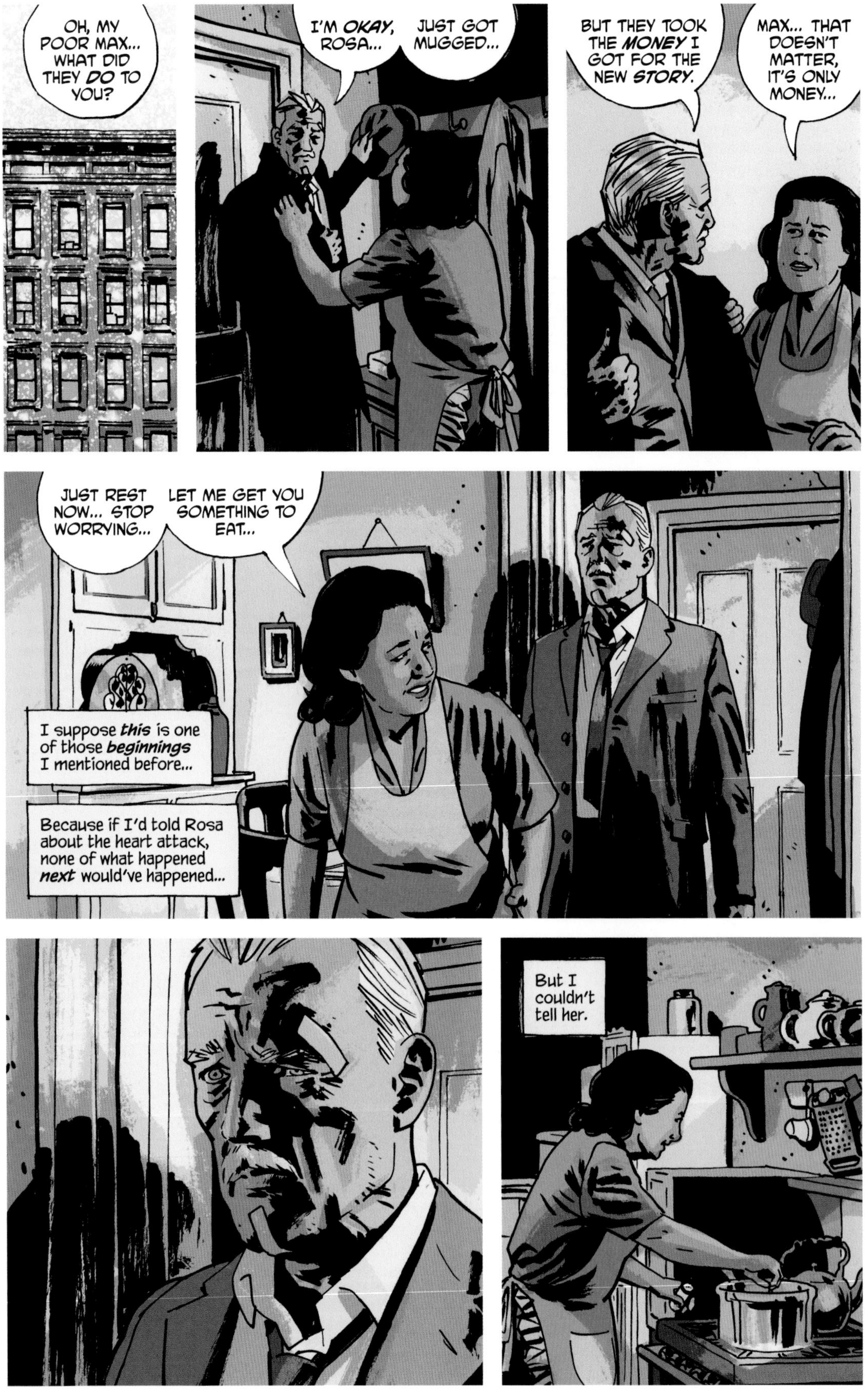
OH, MY POOR MAX... WHAT DID THEY *DO* TO YOU?
I'M *OKAY,* ROSA...
JUST GOT MUGGED...
BUT THEY TOOK THE *MONEY* I GOT FOR THE NEW *STORY.*
MAX... THAT DOESN'T MATTER, IT'S ONLY MONEY...
JUST REST NOW... STOP WORRYING...
LET ME GET YOU SOMETHING TO EAT...
I suppose ***this*** is one of those ***beginnings*** I mentioned before...
Because if I'd told Rosa about the heart attack, none of what happened ***next*** would've happened...
But I couldn't tell her.

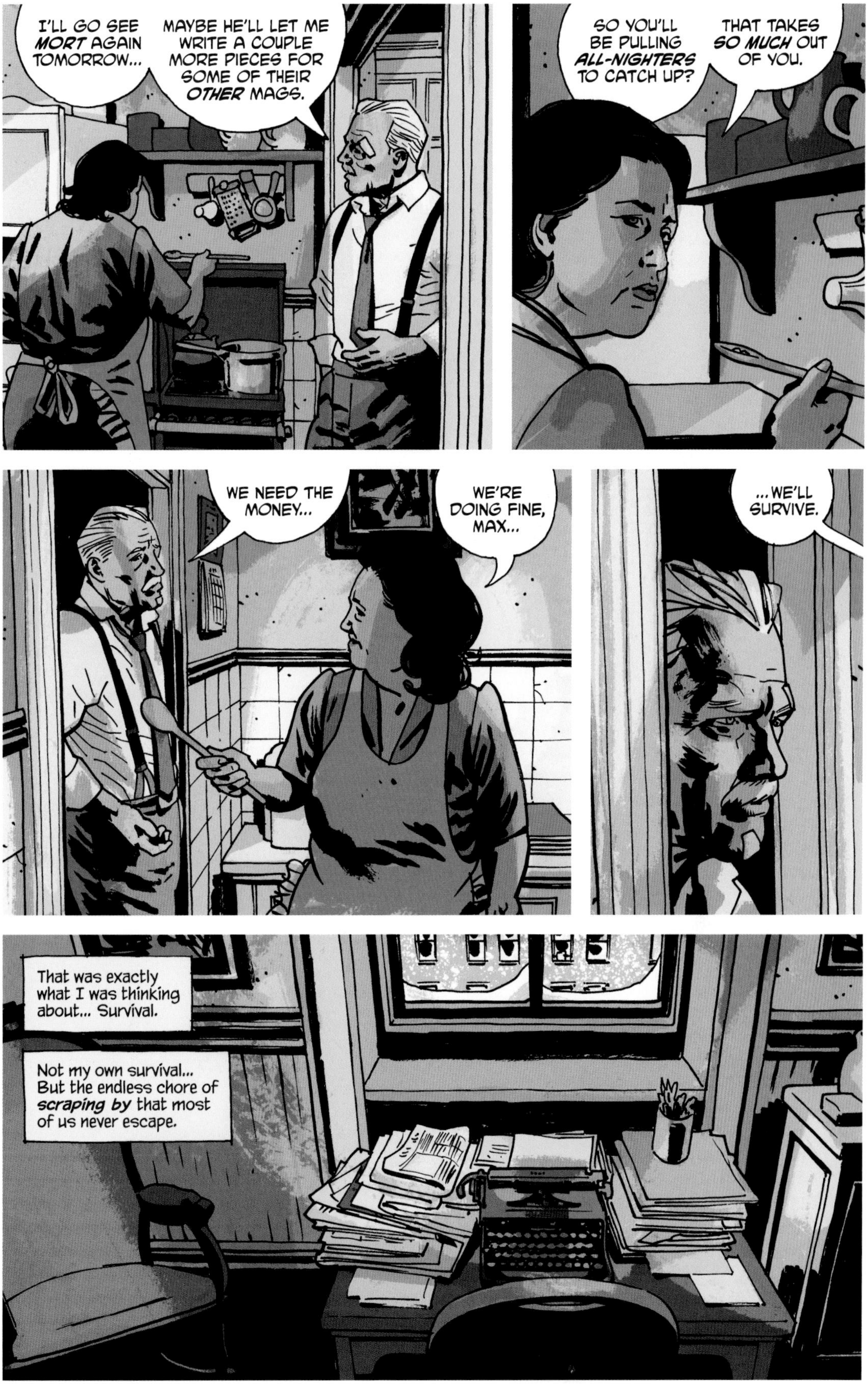
I'LL GO SEE *MORT* AGAIN TOMORROW...
MAYBE HE'LL LET ME WRITE A COUPLE MORE PIECES FOR SOME OF THEIR *OTHER* MAGS.
SO YOU'LL BE PULLING *ALL-NIGHTERS* TO CATCH UP?
THAT TAKES *SO MUCH* OUT OF YOU.
WE NEED THE MONEY...
WE'RE DOING FINE, MAX...
...WE'LL SURVIVE.
That was exactly what I was thinking about... Survival.
Not my own survival... But the endless chore of *scraping by* that most of us never escape.

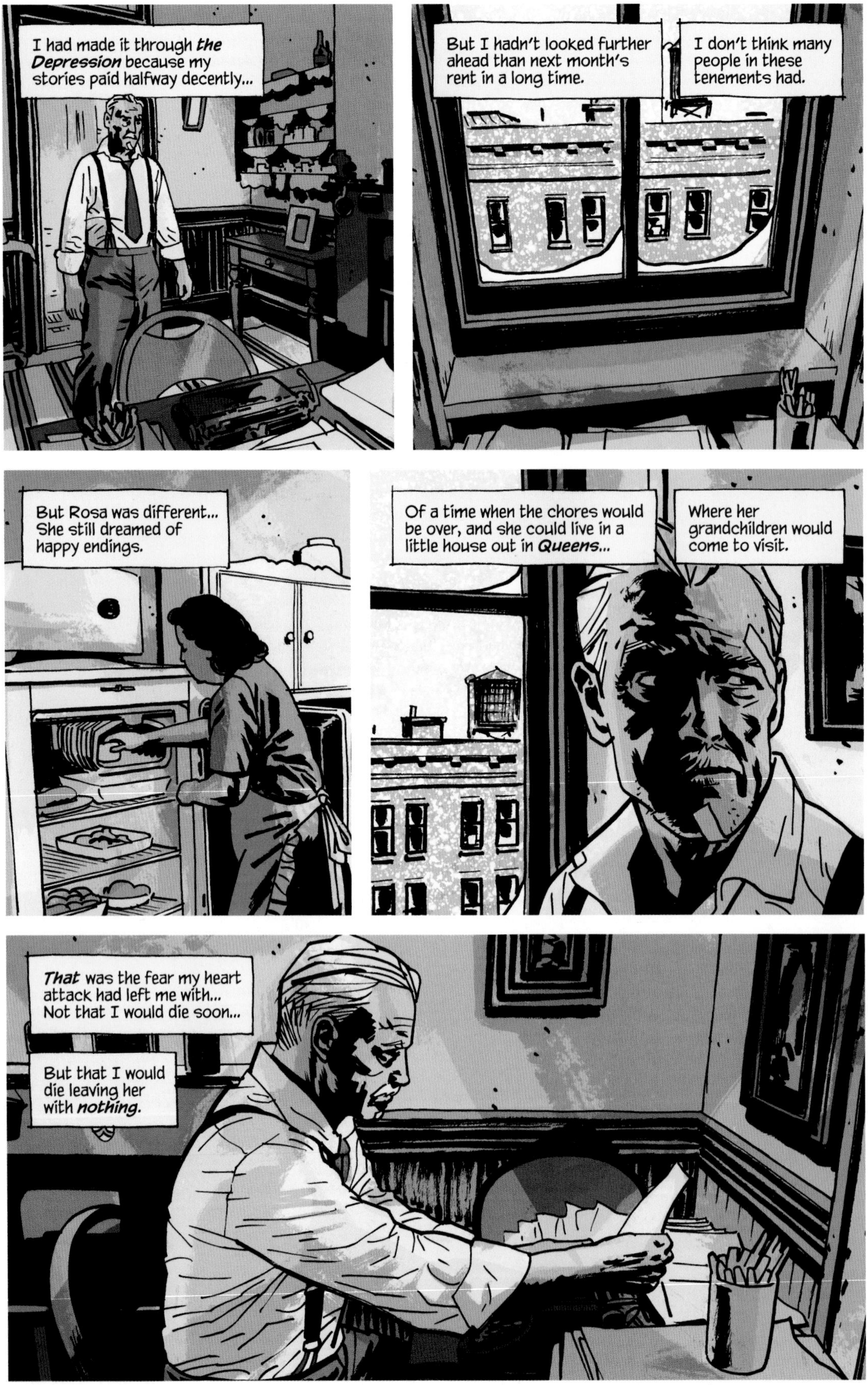
I had made it through *the Depression* because my stories paid halfway decently...
But I hadn't looked further ahead than next month's rent in a long time.
I don't think many people in these tenements had.
But Rosa was different... She still dreamed of happy endings.
Of a time when the chores would be over, and she could live in a little house out in *Queens*...
Where her grandchildren would come to visit.
That was the fear my heart attack had left me with... Not that I would die soon...
But that I would die leaving her with *nothing*.

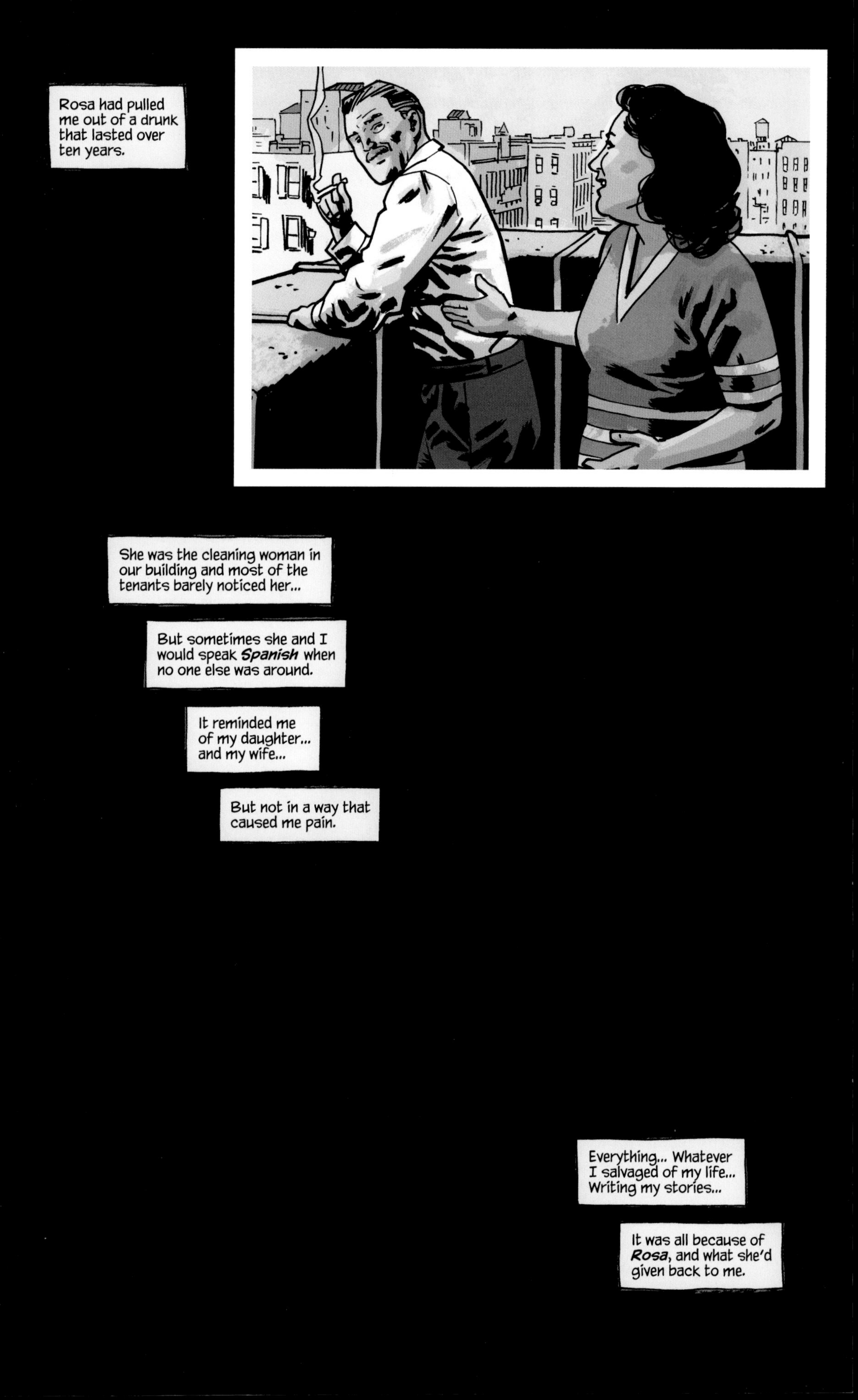
Rosa had pulled me out of a drunk that lasted over ten years.
She was the cleaning woman in our building and most of the tenants barely noticed her...
But sometimes she and I would speak *Spanish* when no one else was around.
It reminded me of my daughter... and my wife...
But not in a way that caused me pain.
Everything... Whatever I salvaged of my life... Writing my stories...
It was all because of *Rosa*, and what she'd given back to me.

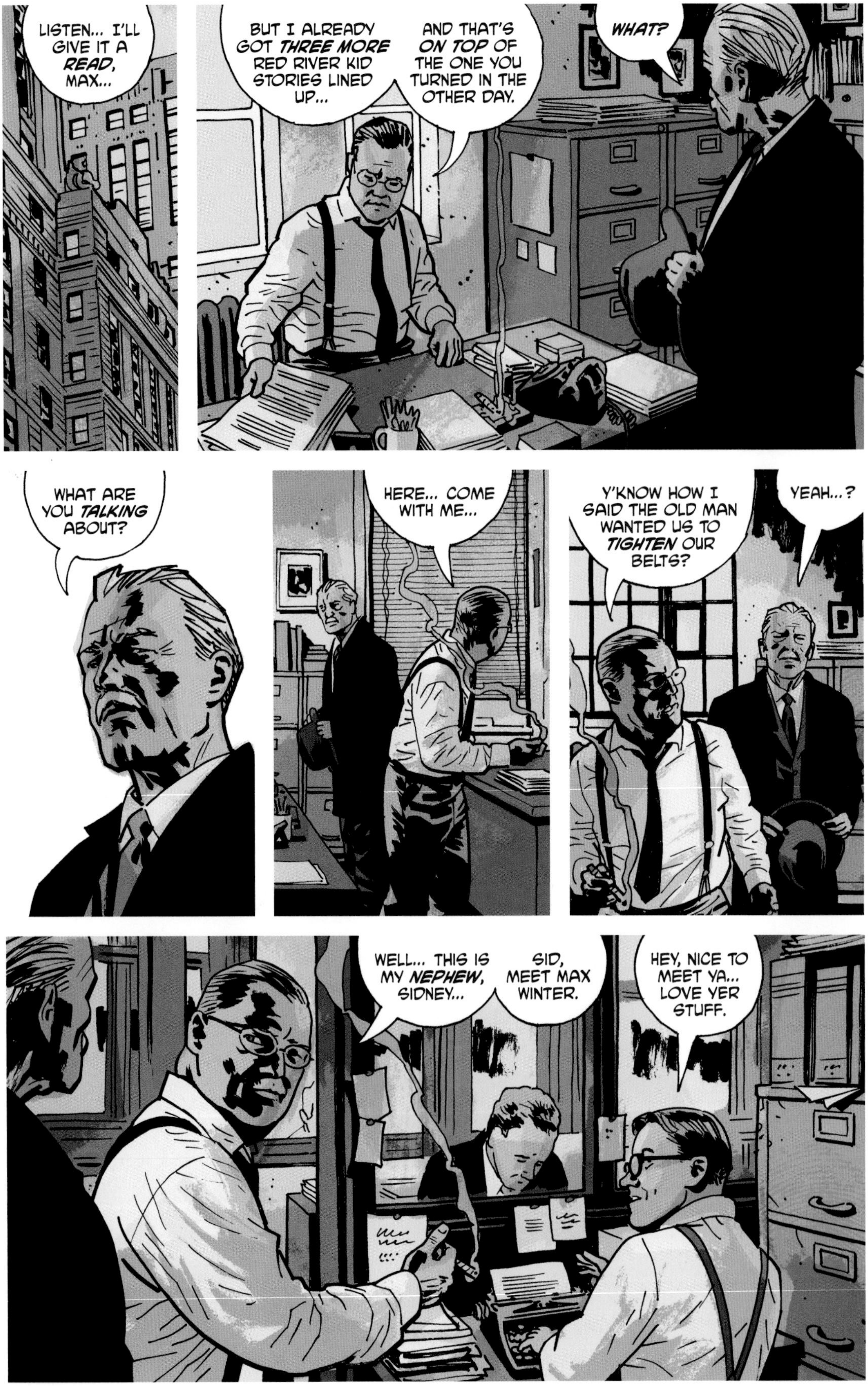
LISTEN... I'LL GIVE IT A READ, MAX...
BUT I ALREADY GOT THREE MORE RED RIVER KID STORIES LINED UP...
AND THAT'S ON TOP OF THE ONE YOU TURNED IN THE OTHER DAY.
WHAT?
WHAT ARE YOU TALKING ABOUT?
HERE... COME WITH ME...
Y'KNOW HOW I SAID THE OLD MAN WANTED US TO TIGHTEN OUR BELTS?
YEAH...?
WELL... THIS IS MY NEPHEW, SIDNEY...
SID, MEET MAX WINTER.
HEY, NICE TO MEET YA... LOVE YER STUFF.

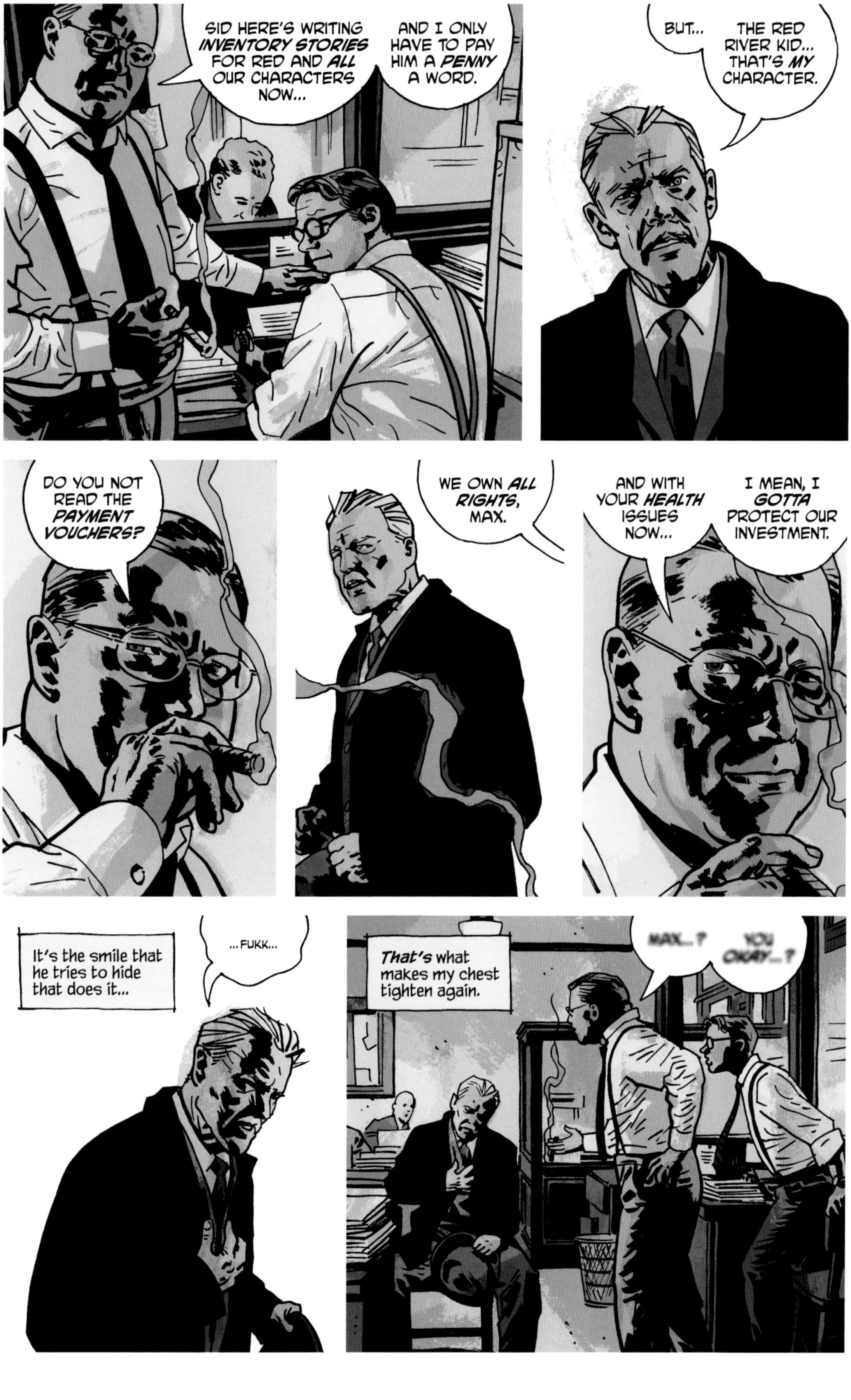
SID HERE'S WRITING INVENTORY STORIES FOR RED AND ALL OUR CHARACTERS NOW...
AND I ONLY HAVE TO PAY HIM A PENNY A WORD.
BUT...
THE RED RIVER KID... THAT'S MY CHARACTER.
DO YOU NOT READ THE PAYMENT VOUCHERS?
WE OWN ALL RIGHTS, MAX.
AND WITH YOUR HEALTH ISSUES NOW...
I MEAN, I GOTTA PROTECT OUR INVESTMENT.
It's the smile that he tries to hide that does it...
...FUKK...
That's what makes my chest tighten again.
MAX...?
YOU OKAY...?

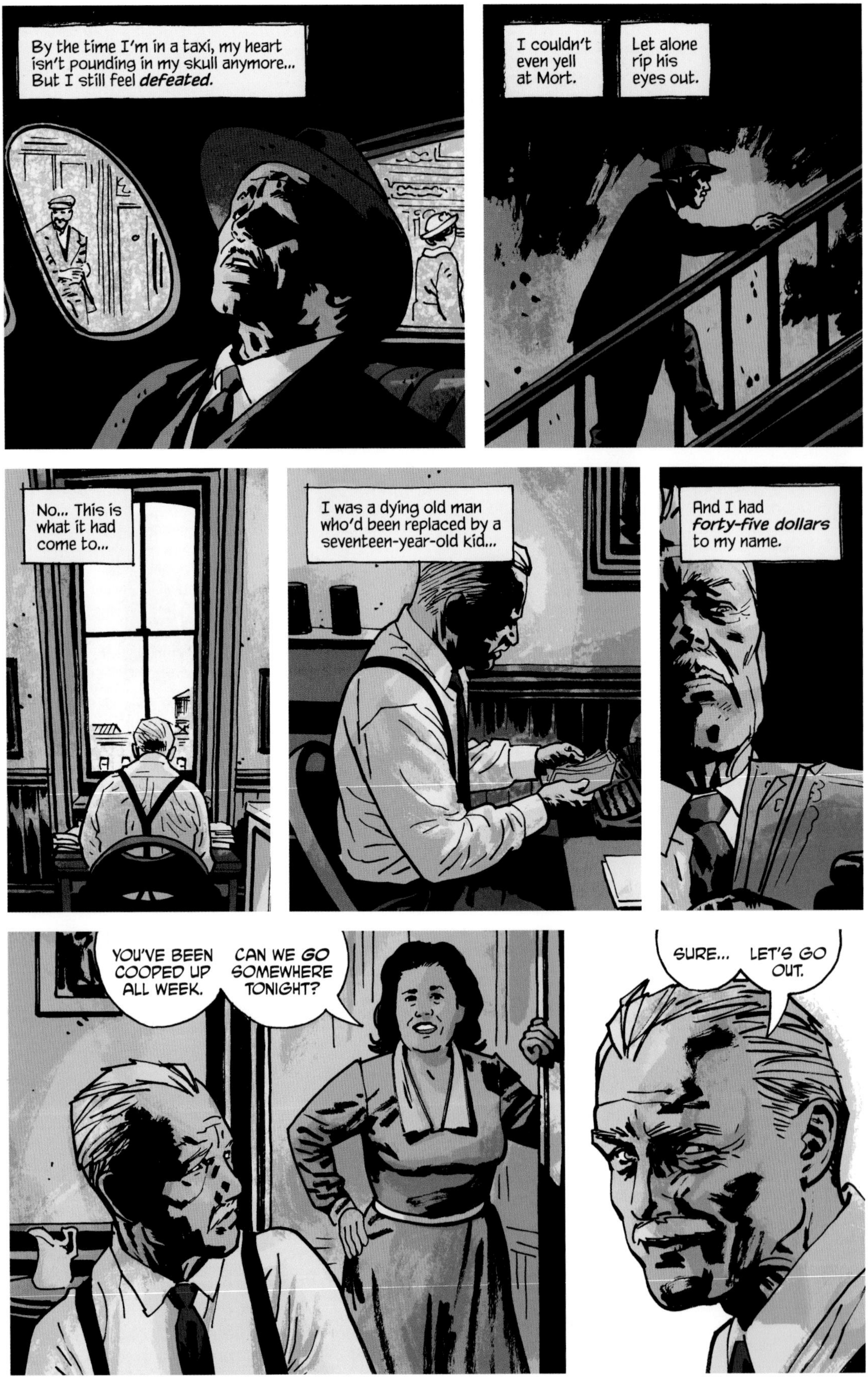
By the time I'm in a taxi, my heart isn't pounding in my skull anymore... But I still feel *defeated.*
I couldn't even yell at Mort.
Let alone rip his eyes out.
No... This is what it had come to...
I was a dying old man who'd been replaced by a seventeen-year-old kid...
And I had *forty-five dollars* to my name.
YOU'VE BEEN COOPED UP ALL WEEK.
CAN WE *GO* SOMEWHERE TONIGHT?
SURE...
LET'S GO OUT.

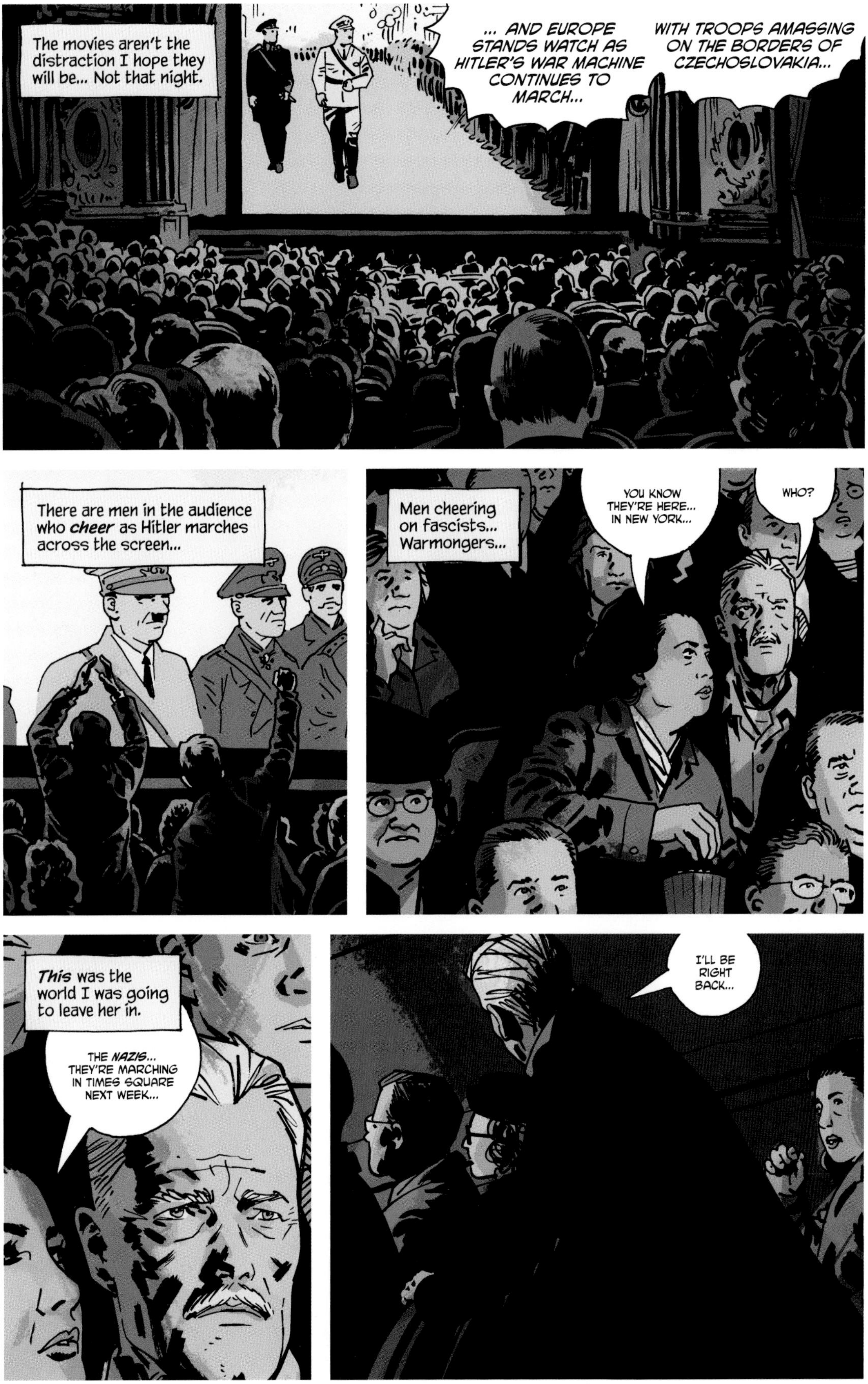

The movies aren't the distraction I hope they will be... Not that night.
... AND EUROPE STANDS WATCH AS HITLER'S WAR MACHINE CONTINUES TO MARCH...
WITH TROOPS AMASSING ON THE BORDERS OF CZECHOSLOVAKIA...
There are men in the audience who *cheer* as Hitler marches across the screen...
Men cheering on fascists... Warmongers...
YOU KNOW THEY'RE HERE... IN NEW YORK...
WHO?
This was the world I was going to leave her in.
THE *NAZIS*... THEY'RE MARCHING IN TIMES SQUARE NEXT WEEK...
I'LL BE RIGHT BACK...

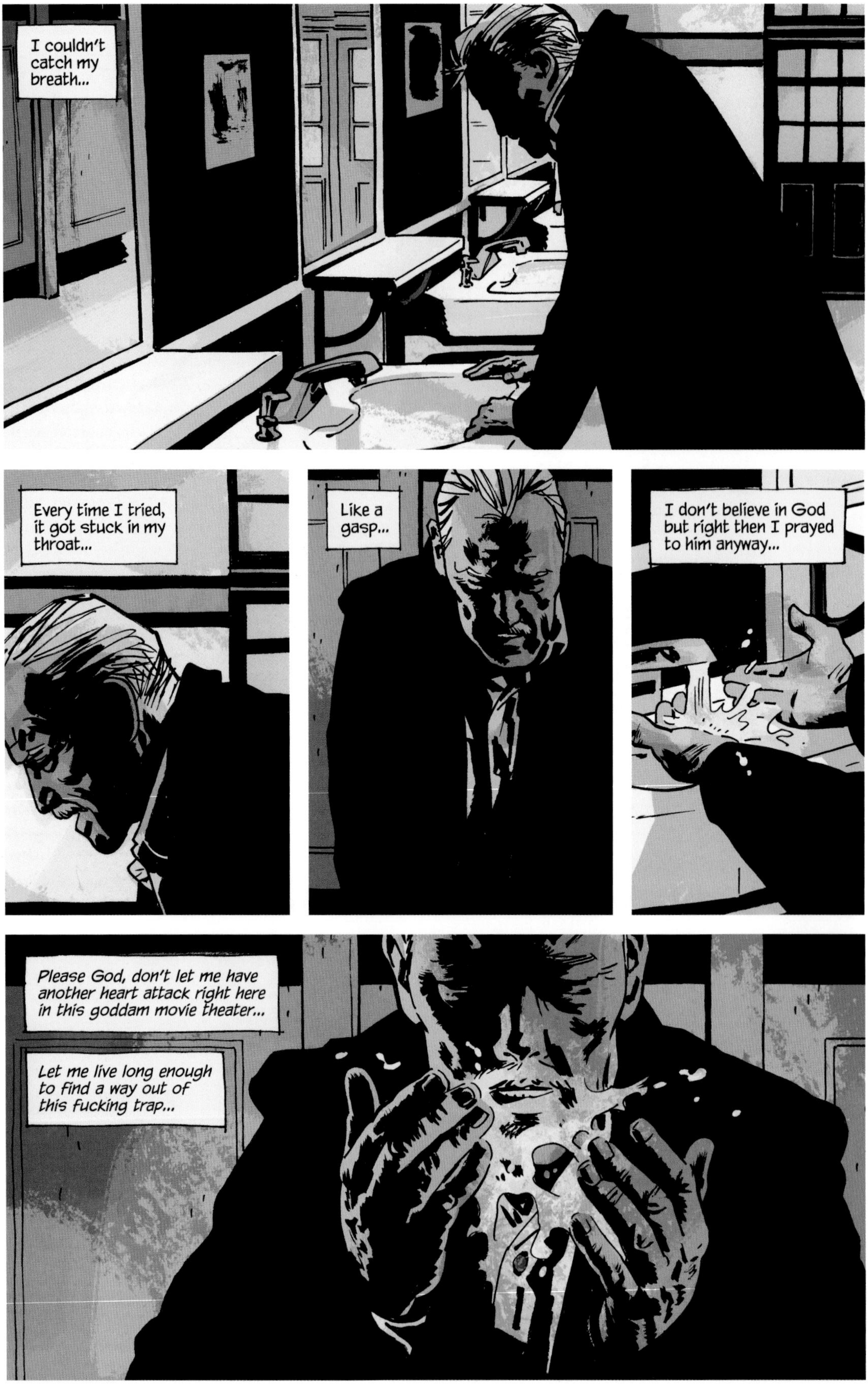
I couldn't catch my breath...
Every time I tried, it got stuck in my throat...
Like a gasp...
I don't believe in God but right then I prayed to him anyway...
Please God, don't let me have another heart attack right here in this goddam movie theater...
Let me live long enough to find a way out of this fucking trap...

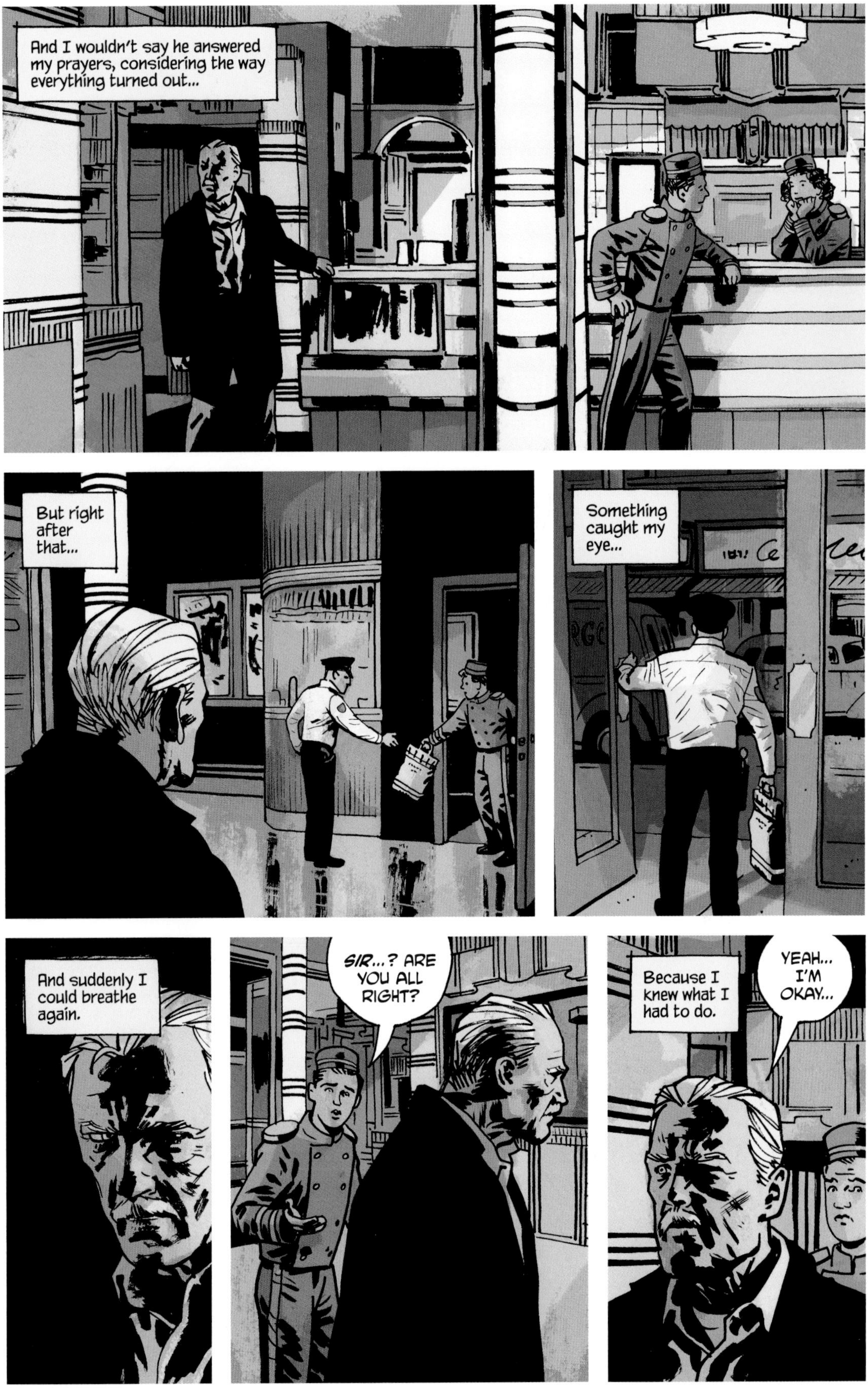
And I wouldn't say he answered my prayers, considering the way everything turned out...
But right after that...
Something caught my eye...
And suddenly I could breathe again.
SIR...? ARE YOU ALL RIGHT?
Because I knew what I had to do.
YEAH... I'M OKAY...

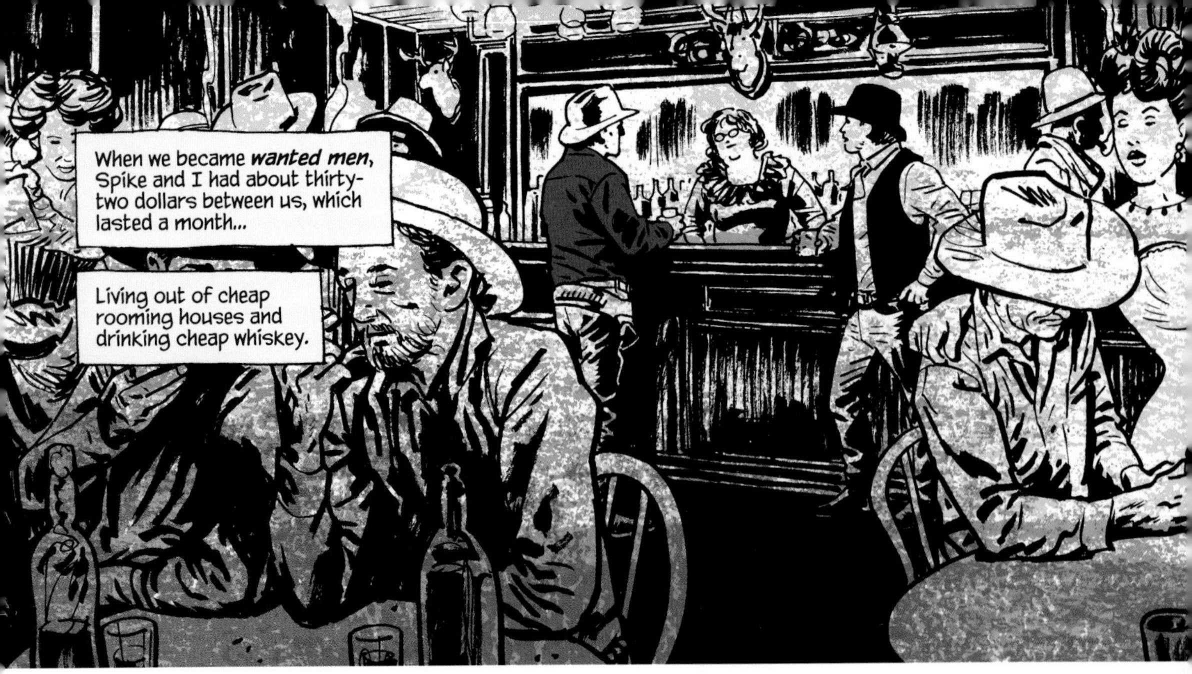
When we became ***wanted men***, Spike and I had about thirty-two dollars between us, which lasted a month...
Living out of cheap rooming houses and drinking cheap whiskey.

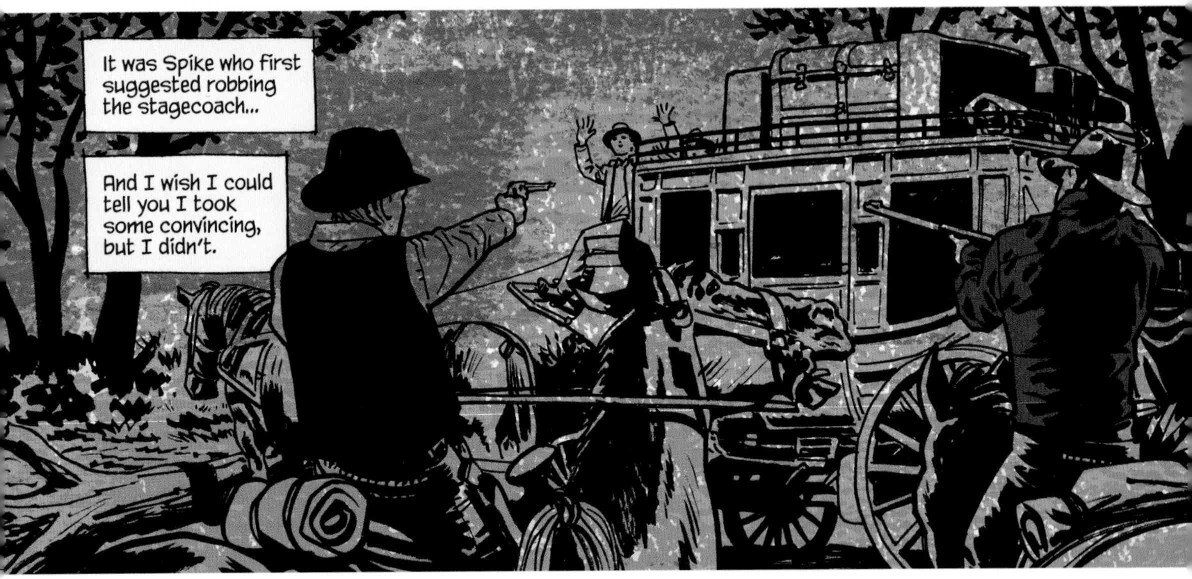
It was Spike who first suggested robbing the stagecoach...
And I wish I could tell you I took some convincing, but I didn't.

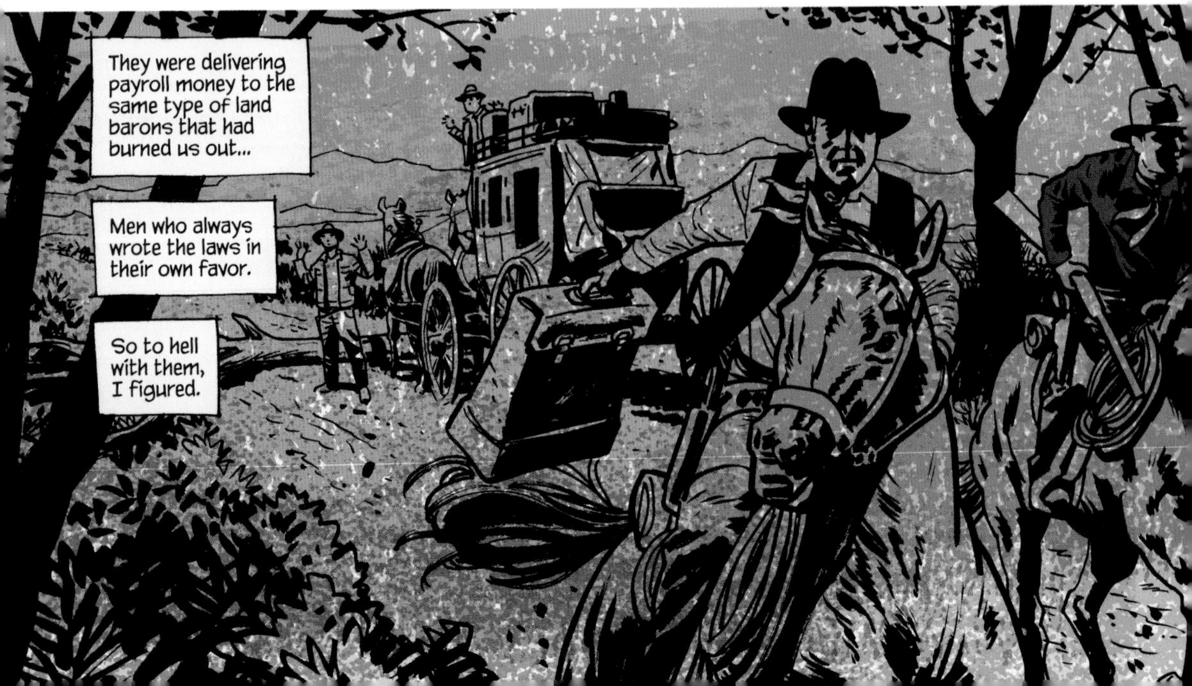
They were delivering payroll money to the same type of land barons that had burned us out...
Men who always wrote the laws in their own favor.
So to hell with them, I figured.

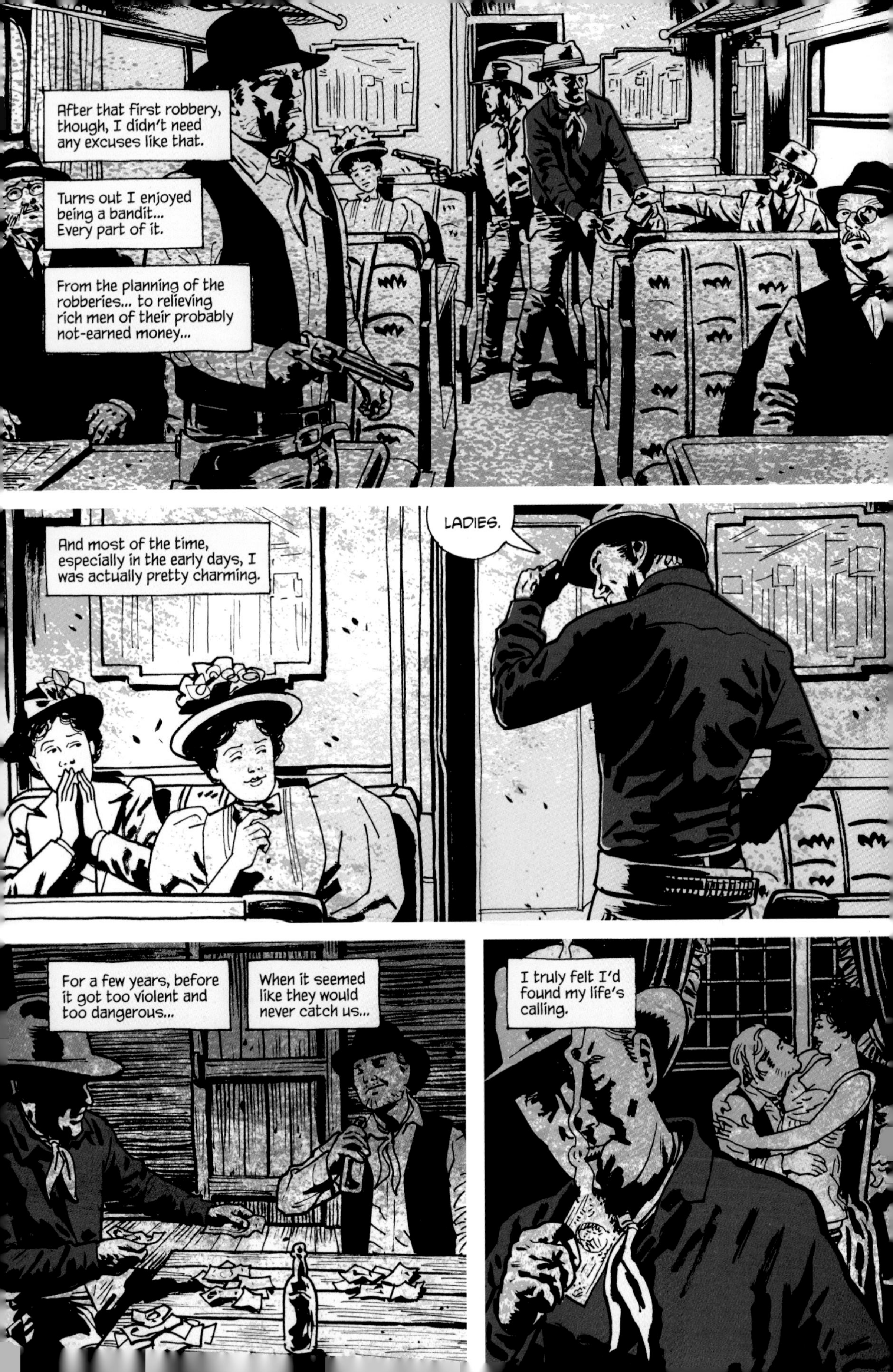
After that first robbery, though, I didn't need any excuses like that.
Turns out I enjoyed being a bandit... Every part of it.
From the planning of the robberies... to relieving rich men of their probably not-earned money...
And most of the time, especially in the early days, I was actually pretty charming.
LADIES.
For a few years, before it got too violent and too dangerous...
When it seemed like they would never catch us...
I truly felt I'd found my life's calling.

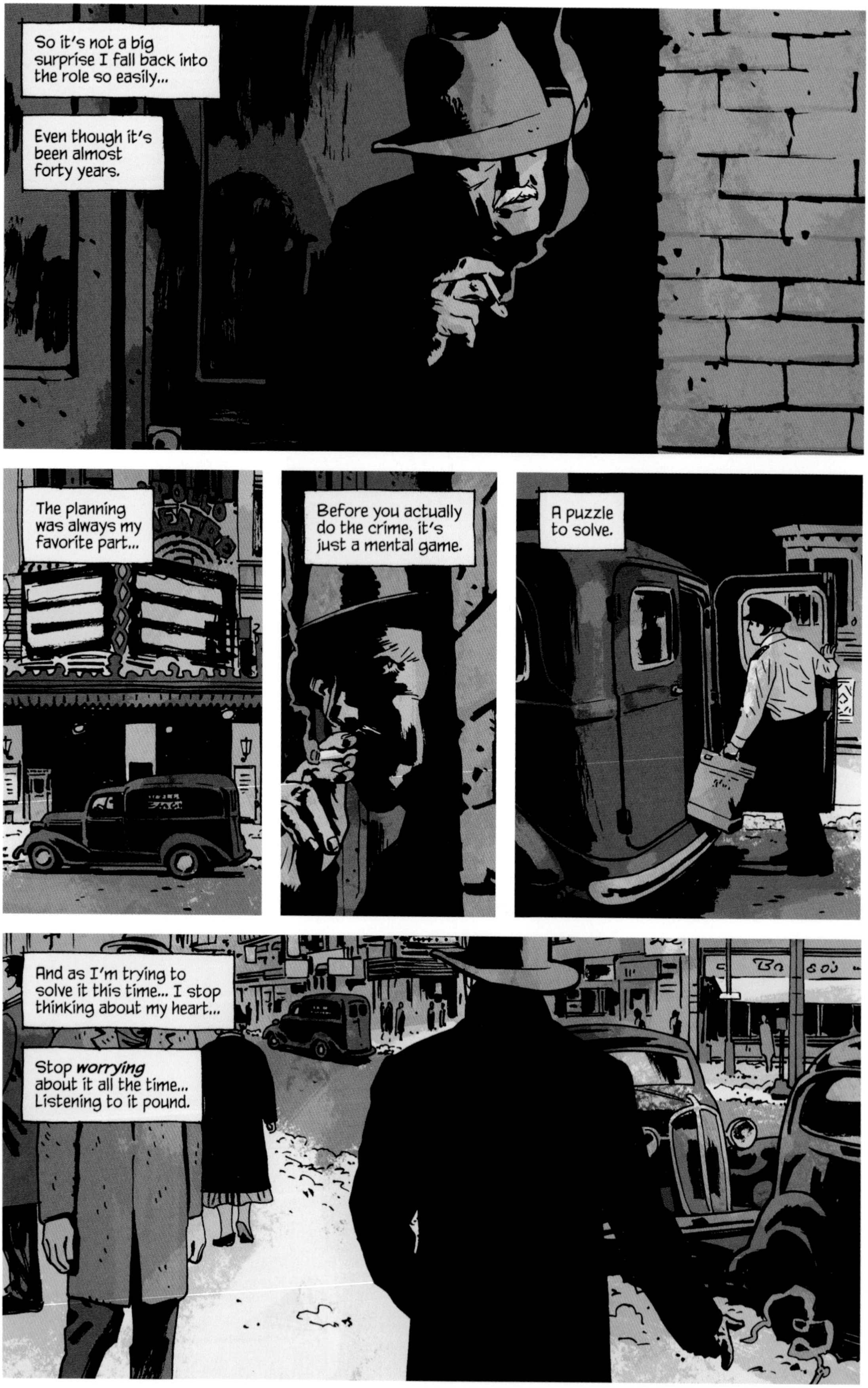
So it's not a big surprise I fall back into the role so easily...
Even though it's been almost forty years.
The planning was always my favorite part...
Before you actually do the crime, it's just a mental game.
A puzzle to solve.
And as I'm trying to solve it this time... I stop thinking about my heart...
Stop *worrying* about it all the time... Listening to it pound.

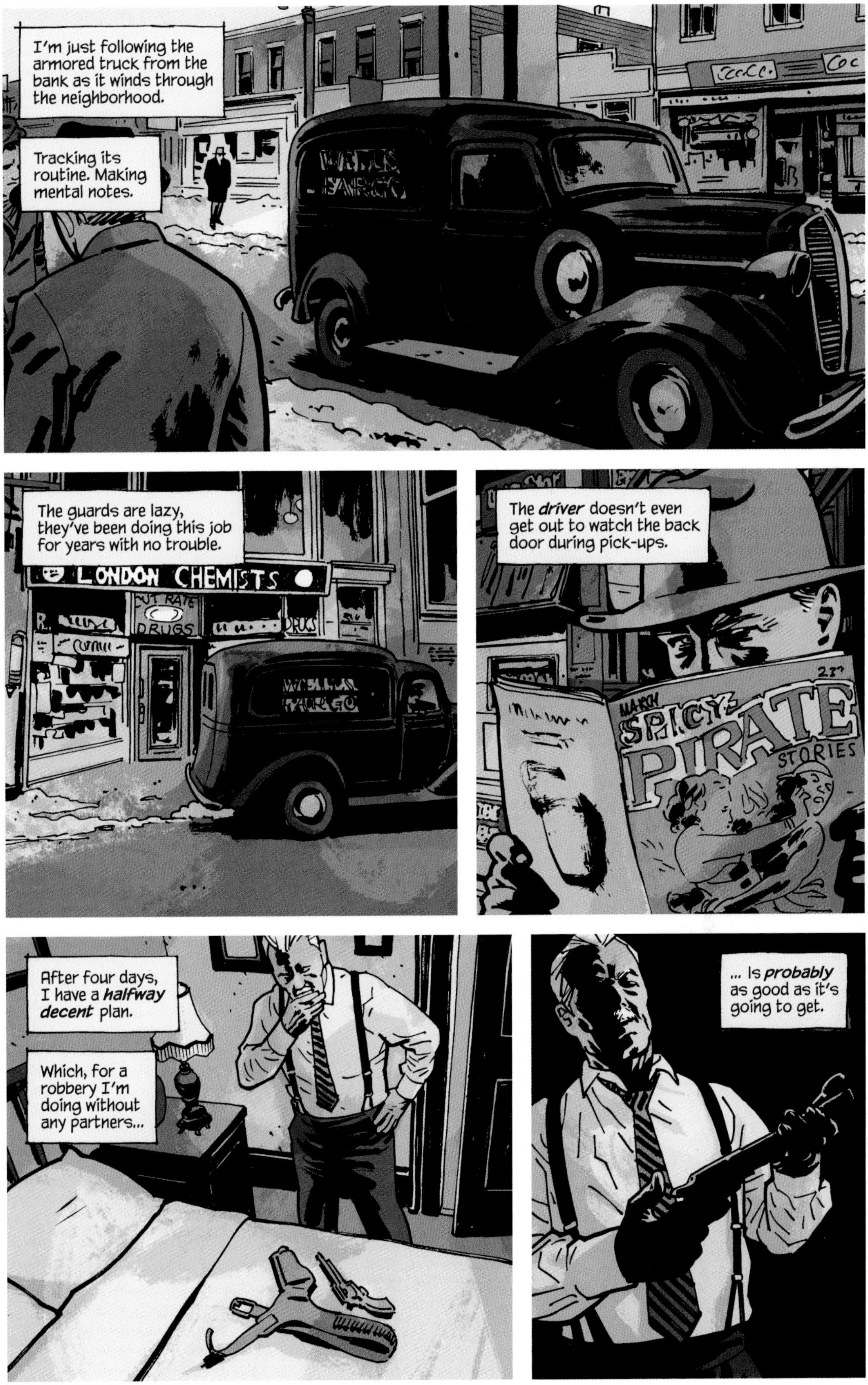

I'm just following the armored truck from the bank as it winds through the neighborhood.
Tracking its routine. Making mental notes.
WELLS FARGO
The guards are lazy, they've been doing this job for years with no trouble.
LONDON CHEMISTS
CUT RATE DRUGS
The *driver* doesn't even get out to watch the back door during pick-ups.
SPICY PIRATE STORIES
MARCH
After four days, I have a ***halfway decent*** plan.
Which, for a robbery I'm doing without any partners...
... Is ***probably*** as good as it's going to get.

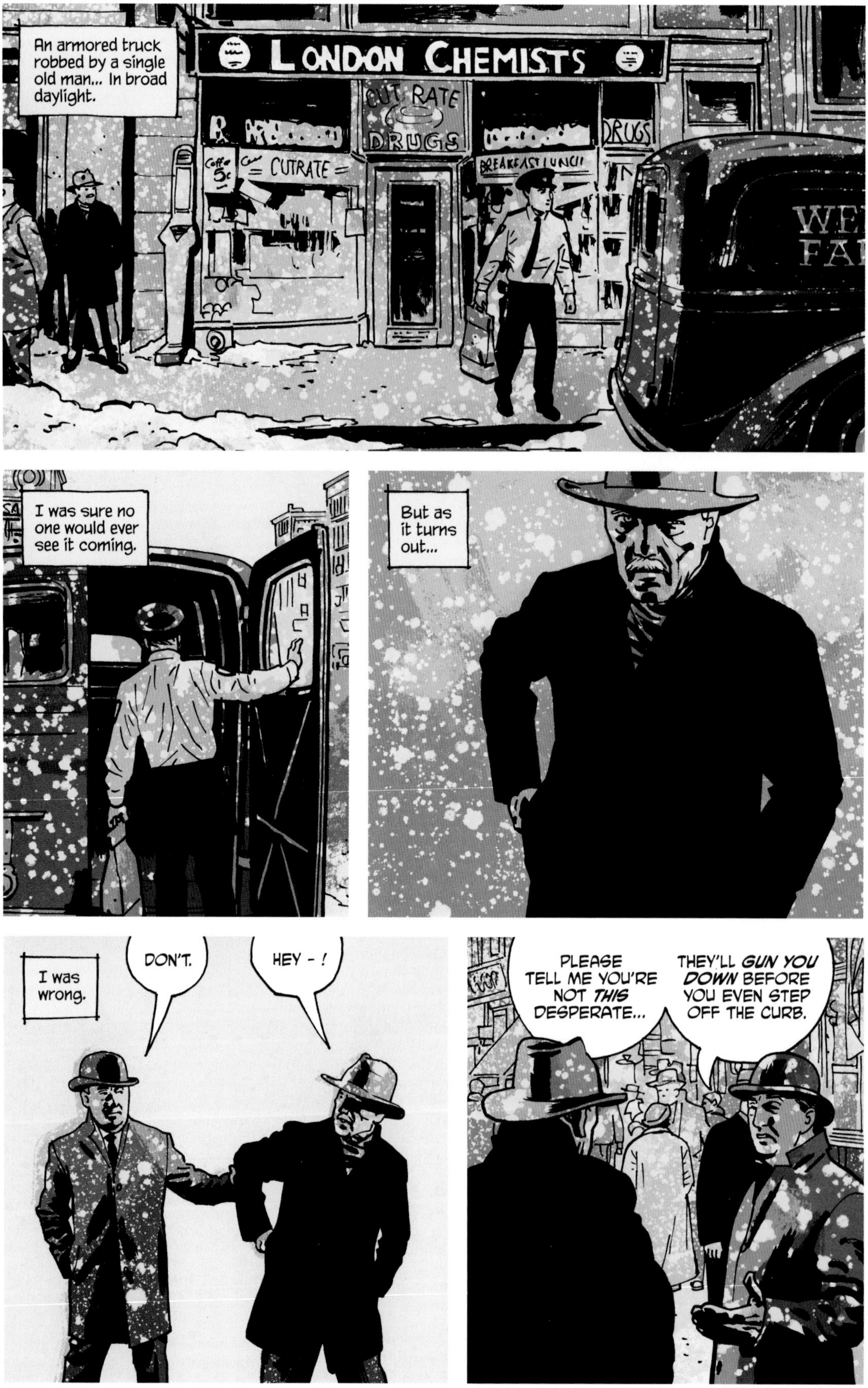
An armored truck robbed by a single old man... In broad daylight.
LONDON CHEMISTS
CUT RATE DRUGS
CUTRATE
DRUGS
BREAKFAST LUNCH
I was sure no one would ever see it coming.
But as it turns out...
I was wrong.
DON'T.
HEY - !
PLEASE TELL ME YOU'RE NOT *THIS* DESPERATE...
THEY'LL ***GUN YOU DOWN*** BEFORE YOU EVEN STEP OFF THE CURB.

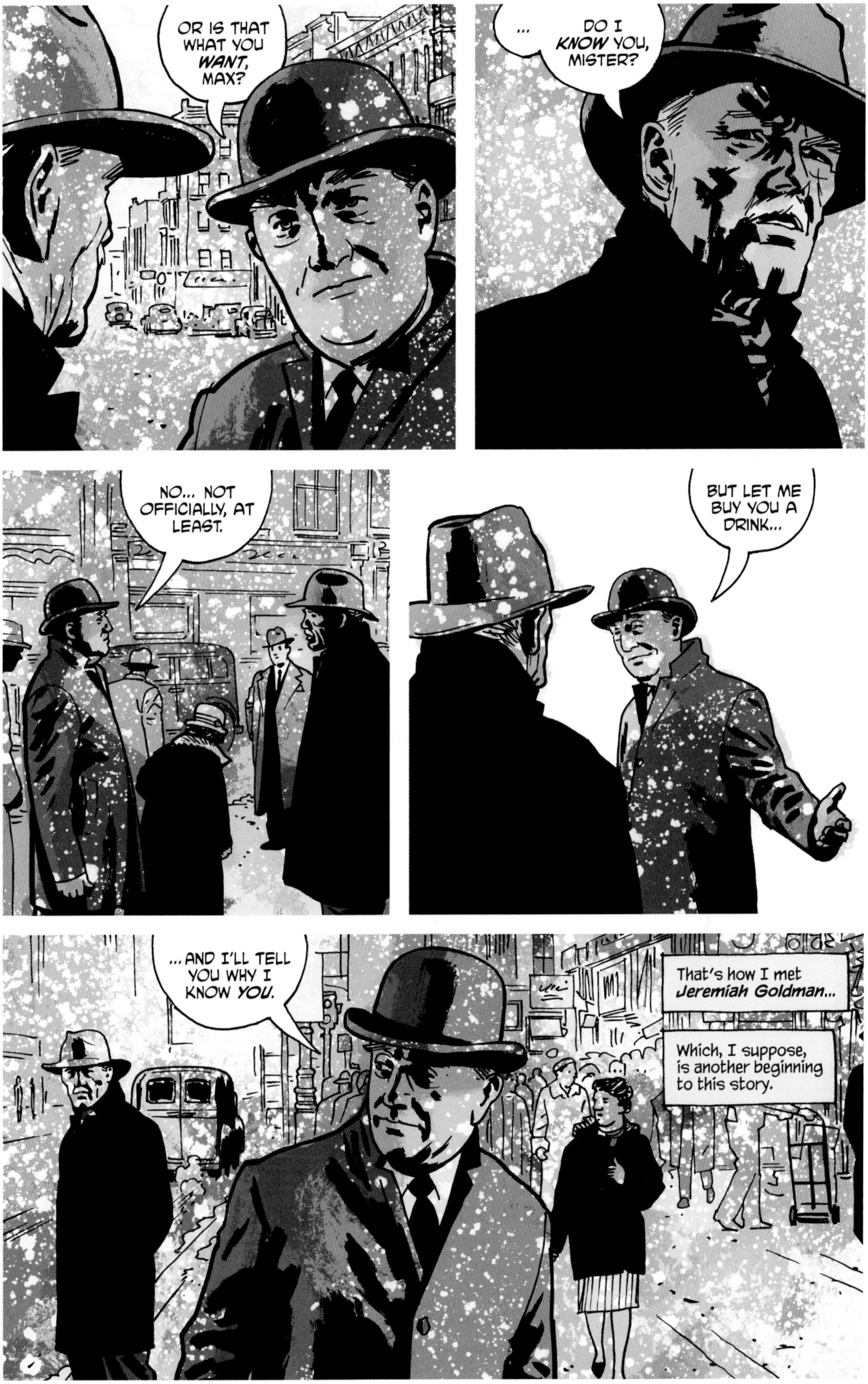
OR IS THAT WHAT YOU *WANT,* MAX?
... DO I *KNOW* YOU, MISTER?
NO... NOT OFFICIALLY, AT LEAST.
BUT LET ME BUY YOU A DRINK...
...AND I'LL TELL YOU WHY I KNOW *YOU.*
That's how I met *Jeremiah Goldman...*
Which, I suppose, is another beginning to this story.

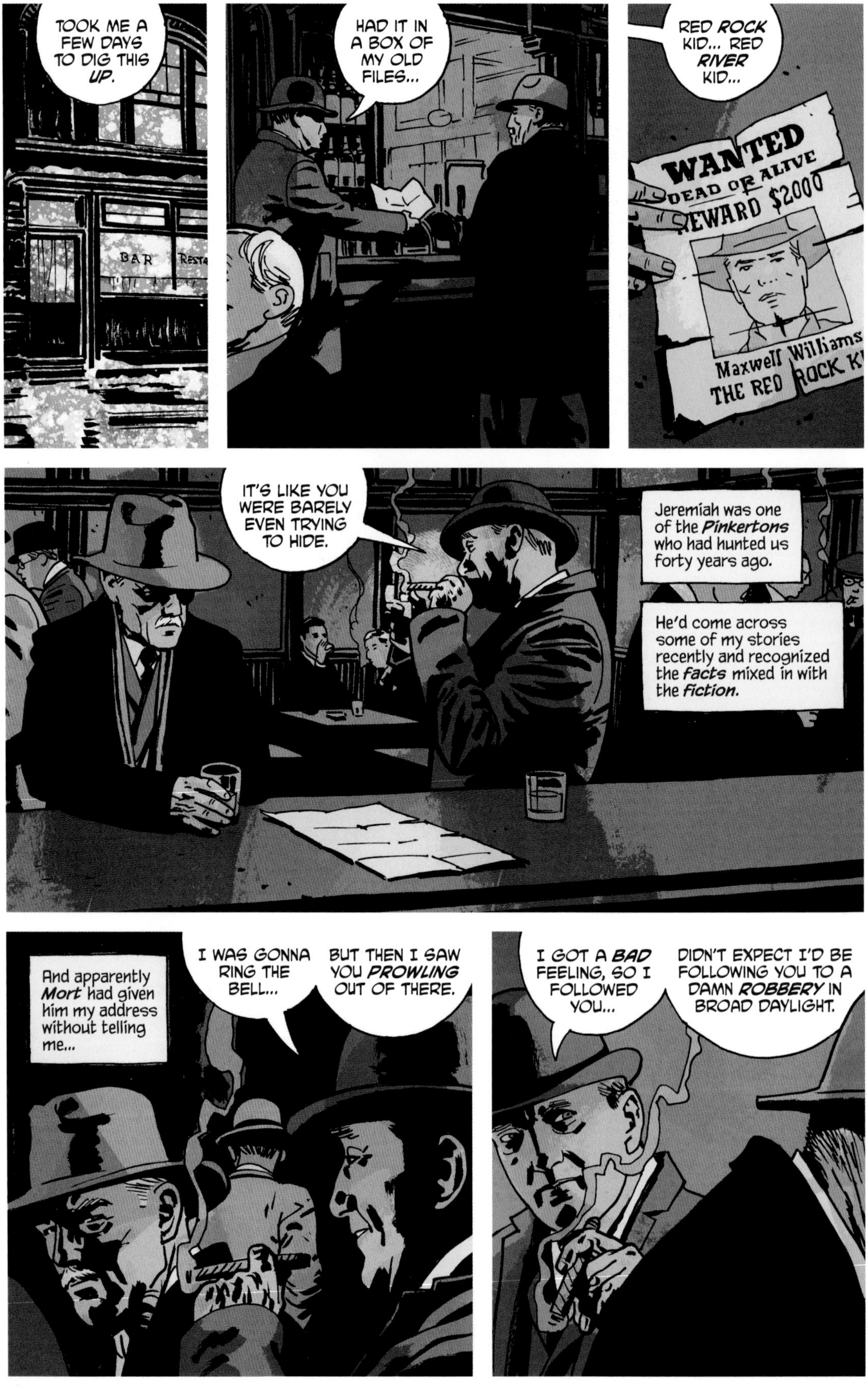
TOOK ME A FEW DAYS TO DIG THIS *UP*.
HAD IT IN A BOX OF MY OLD FILES...
RED *ROCK* KID... RED *RIVER* KID...
WANTED
DEAD OR ALIVE
REWARD $2000
Maxwell Williams
THE RED ROCK KI
IT'S LIKE YOU WERE BARELY EVEN TRYING TO HIDE.
Jeremiah was one of the *Pinkertons* who had hunted us forty years ago.
He'd come across some of my stories recently and recognized the *facts* mixed in with the *fiction*.
And apparently *Mort* had given him my address without telling me...
I WAS GONNA RING THE BELL...
BUT THEN I SAW YOU *PROWLING* OUT OF THERE.
I GOT A *BAD* FEELING, SO I FOLLOWED YOU...
DIDN'T EXPECT I'D BE FOLLOWING YOU TO A DAMN *ROBBERY* IN BROAD DAYLIGHT.

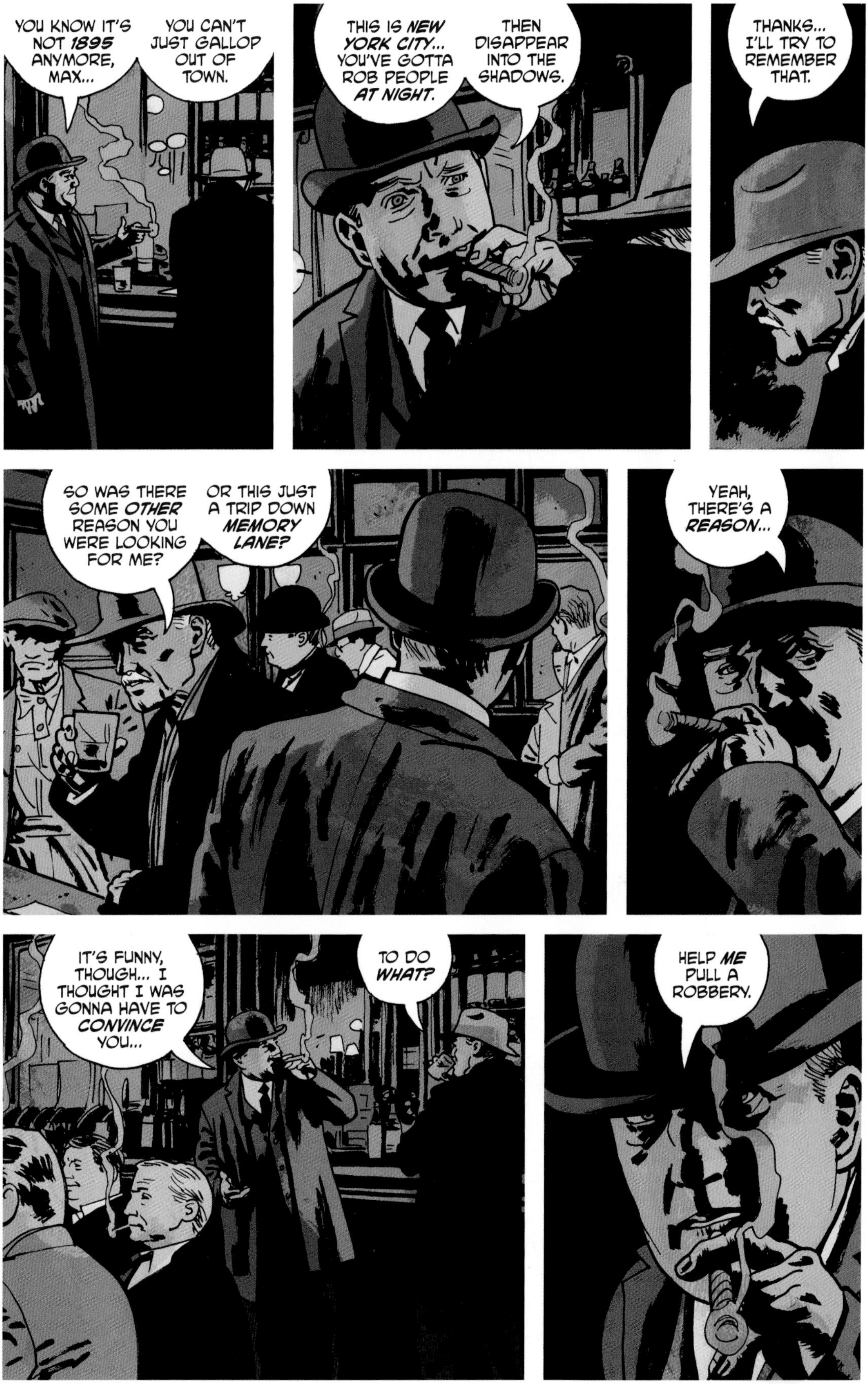
YOU KNOW IT'S NOT *1895* ANYMORE, MAX...
YOU CAN'T JUST GALLOP OUT OF TOWN.
THIS IS *NEW YORK CITY*... YOU'VE GOTTA ROB PEOPLE *AT NIGHT*.
THEN DISAPPEAR INTO THE SHADOWS.
THANKS... I'LL TRY TO REMEMBER THAT.
SO WAS THERE SOME *OTHER* REASON YOU WERE LOOKING FOR ME?
OR THIS JUST A TRIP DOWN *MEMORY LANE?*
YEAH, THERE'S A *REASON*...
IT'S FUNNY, THOUGH... I THOUGHT I WAS GONNA HAVE TO *CONVINCE* YOU...
TO DO *WHAT?*
HELP *ME* PULL A ROBBERY.

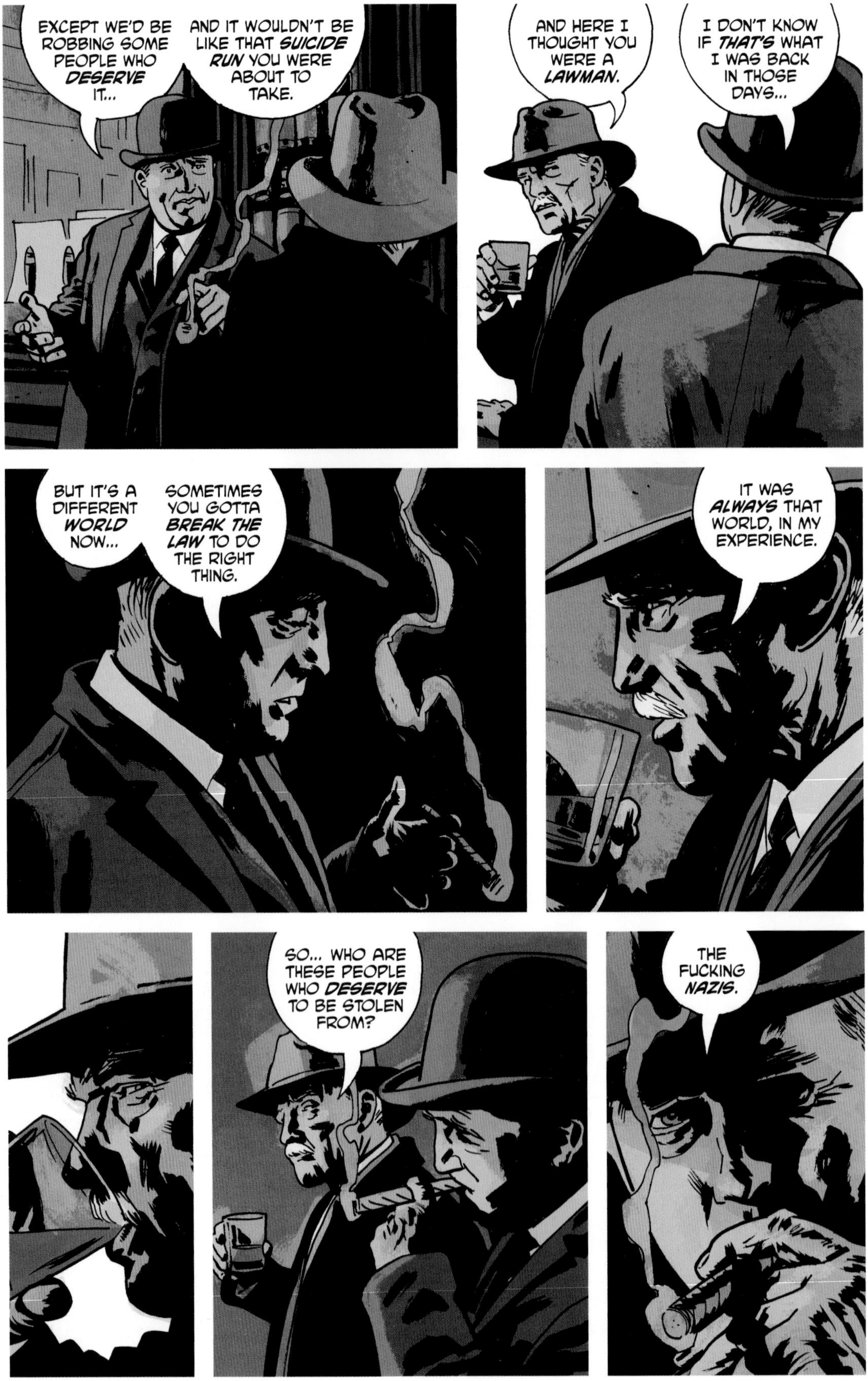
EXCEPT WE'D BE ROBBING SOME PEOPLE WHO *DESERVE* IT...
AND IT WOULDN'T BE LIKE THAT *SUICIDE RUN* YOU WERE ABOUT TO TAKE.
AND HERE I THOUGHT YOU WERE A *LAWMAN*.
I DON'T KNOW IF *THAT'S* WHAT I WAS BACK IN THOSE DAYS...
BUT IT'S A DIFFERENT *WORLD* NOW...
SOMETIMES YOU GOTTA *BREAK THE LAW* TO DO THE RIGHT THING.
IT WAS *ALWAYS* THAT WORLD, IN MY EXPERIENCE.
SO... WHO ARE THESE PEOPLE WHO *DESERVE* TO BE STOLEN FROM?
THE FUCKING *NAZIS*.

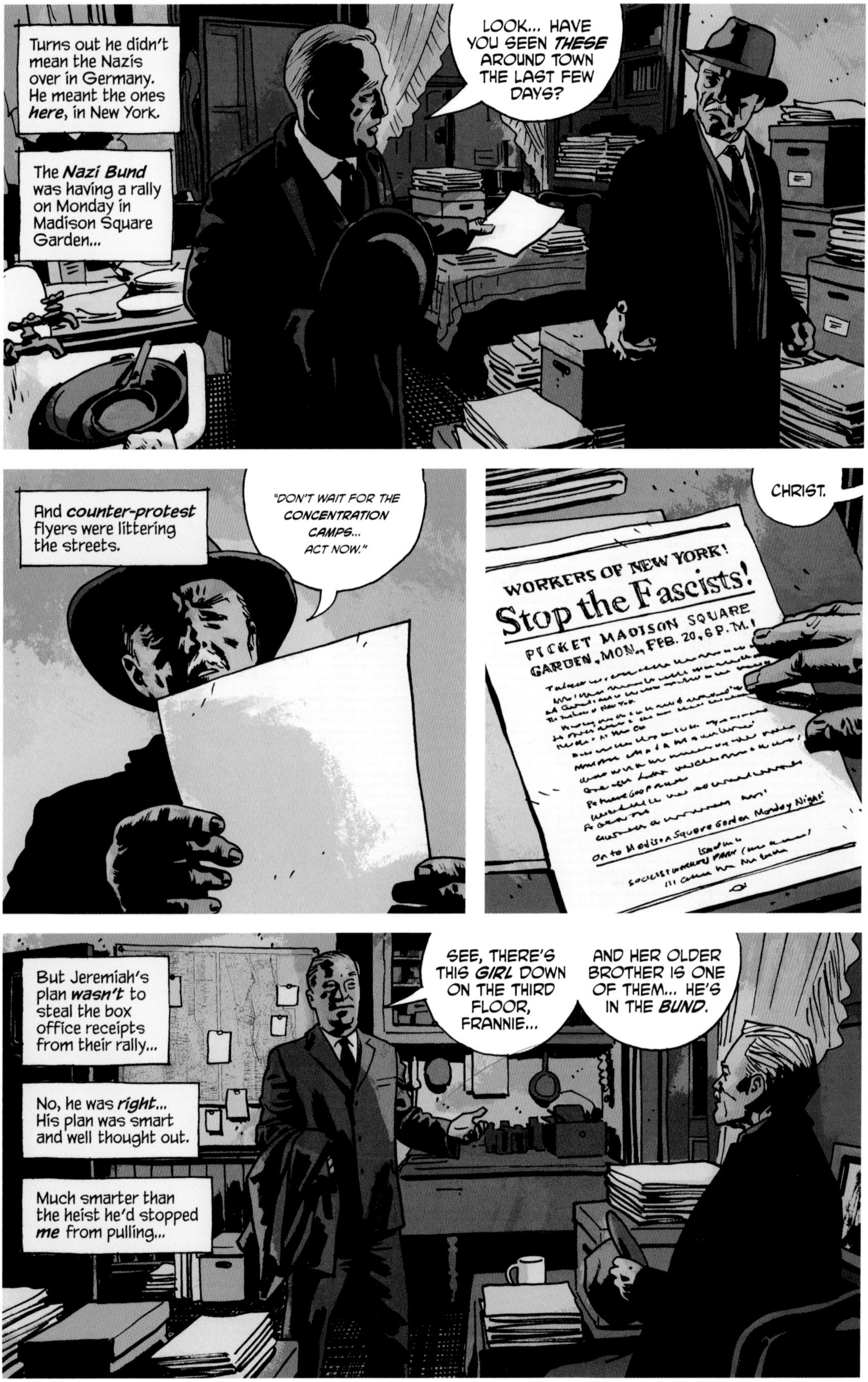

Turns out he didn't mean the Nazis over in Germany. He meant the ones *here*, in New York.
The *Nazi Bund* was having a rally on Monday in Madison Square Garden...
LOOK... HAVE YOU SEEN *THESE* AROUND TOWN THE LAST FEW DAYS?
And *counter-protest* flyers were littering the streets.
"DON'T WAIT FOR THE CONCENTRATION CAMPS... ACT NOW."
CHRIST.
WORKERS OF NEW YORK!
Stop the Fascists!
PICKET MADISON SQUARE GARDEN, MON., FEB. 20, 6 P.M.!
On to Madison Square Garden Monday Night!
But Jeremiah's plan *wasn't* to steal the box office receipts from their rally...
No, he was *right*... His plan was smart and well thought out.
Much smarter than the heist he'd stopped *me* from pulling...
SEE, THERE'S THIS *GIRL* DOWN ON THE THIRD FLOOR, FRANNIE...
AND HER OLDER BROTHER IS ONE OF THEM... HE'S IN THE *BUND*.

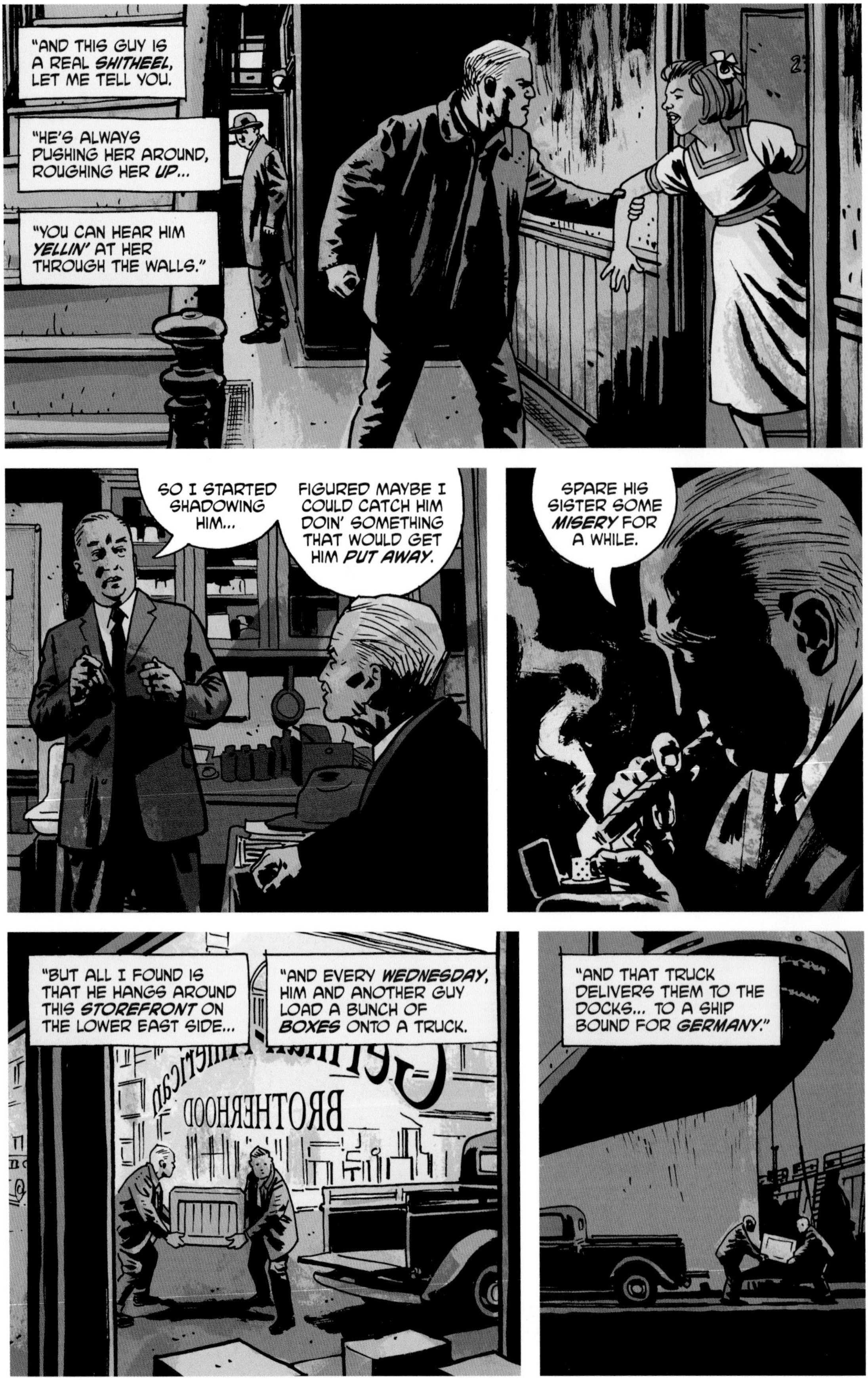

"AND THIS GUY IS A REAL SHITHEEL, LET ME TELL YOU.
"HE'S ALWAYS PUSHING HER AROUND, ROUGHING HER UP...
"YOU CAN HEAR HIM YELLIN' AT HER THROUGH THE WALLS."
SO I STARTED SHADOWING HIM...
FIGURED MAYBE I COULD CATCH HIM DOIN' SOMETHING THAT WOULD GET HIM PUT AWAY.
SPARE HIS SISTER SOME MISERY FOR A WHILE.
"BUT ALL I FOUND IS THAT HE HANGS AROUND THIS STOREFRONT ON THE LOWER EAST SIDE...
"AND EVERY WEDNESDAY, HIM AND ANOTHER GUY LOAD A BUNCH OF BOXES ONTO A TRUCK.
"AND THAT TRUCK DELIVERS THEM TO THE DOCKS... TO A SHIP BOUND FOR GERMANY."

SO I PAID A CONTACT AT *MA BELL* TO LET ME LISTEN IN ON THIS STORE'S *PHONE CALLS*...

AND IT TURNS OUT WHAT THEY'RE SHIPPING IS *CASH.*

THEY GOT PEOPLE ALL OVER AMERICA SENDING MONEY TO HELP FUND THAT MOTHERFUCKER HITLER.

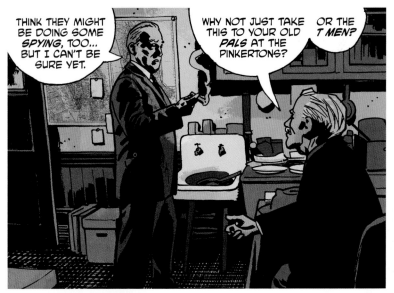

THINK THEY MIGHT BE DOING SOME *SPYING,* TOO... BUT I CAN'T BE SURE YET.

WHY NOT JUST TAKE THIS TO YOUR OLD *PALS* AT THE PINKERTONS?

OR THE *T MEN?*

BECAUSE NONE OF THEM GIVE A SHIT WHAT I HAVE TO SAY ANYMORE.

YOU'RE THE *ONLY ONE* LISTENING TO ME, MAX...

AT LEAST UNTIL I FIND SOME EVIDENCE.

SO HOW ABOUT IT... ARE YOU *IN?*

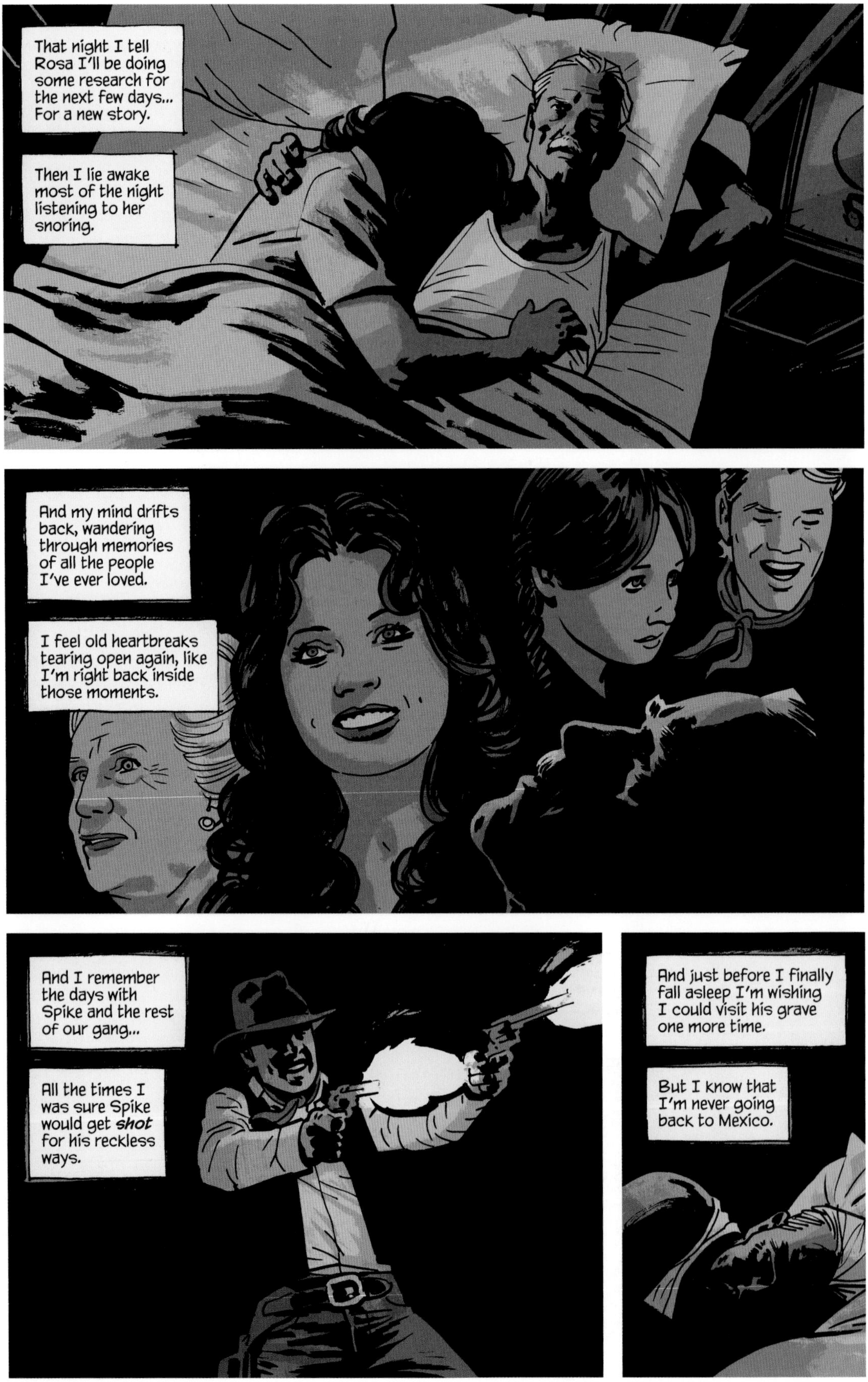
That night I tell Rosa I'll be doing some research for the next few days... For a new story.
Then I lie awake most of the night listening to her snoring.
And my mind drifts back, wandering through memories of all the people I've ever loved.
I feel old heartbreaks tearing open again, like I'm right back inside those moments.
And I remember the days with Spike and the rest of our gang...
All the times I was sure Spike would get ***shot*** for his reckless ways.
And just before I finally fall asleep I'm wishing I could visit his grave one more time.
But I know that I'm never going back to Mexico.

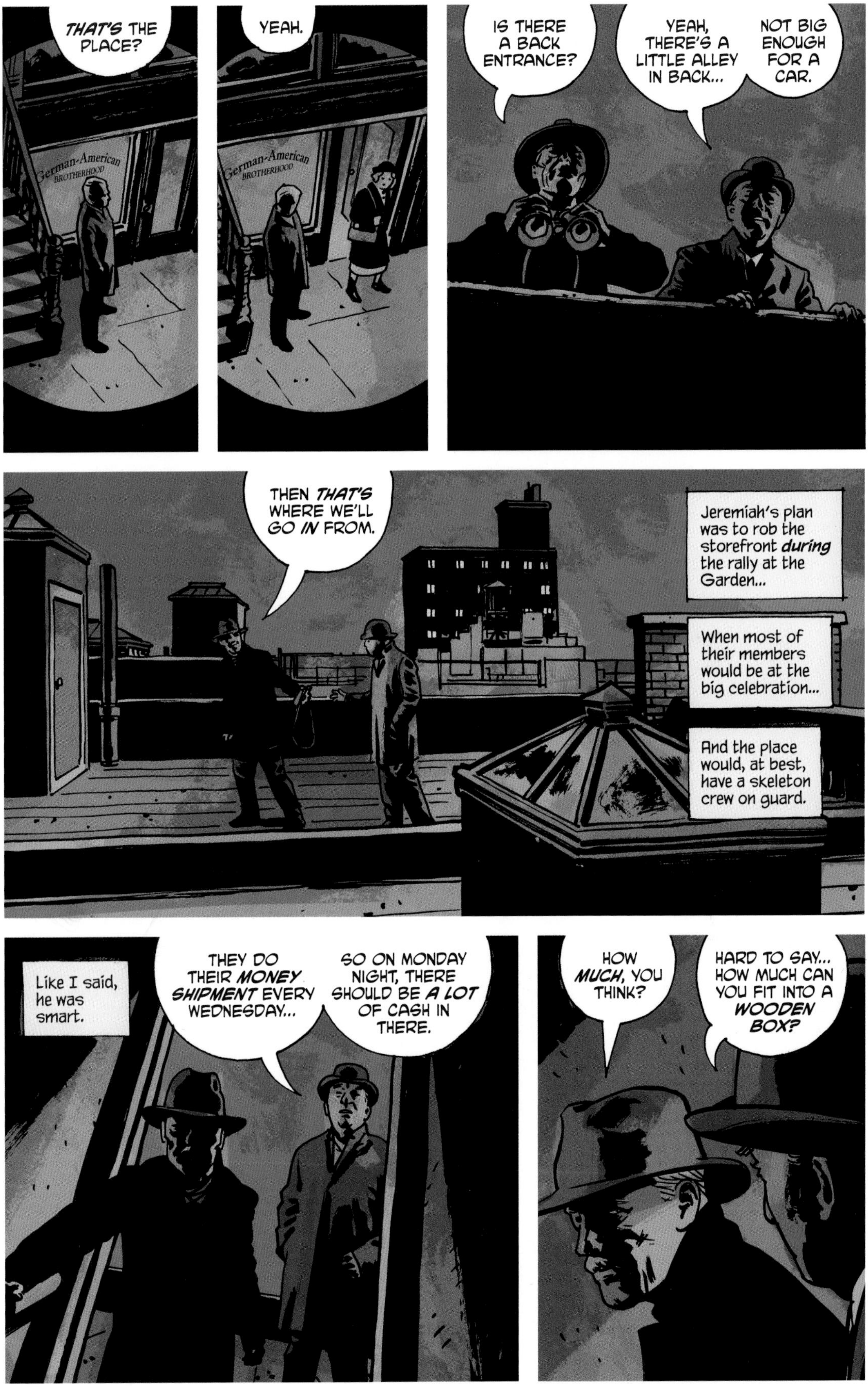
THAT'S THE PLACE?
YEAH.
IS THERE A BACK ENTRANCE?
YEAH, THERE'S A LITTLE ALLEY IN BACK...
NOT BIG ENOUGH FOR A CAR.
THEN THAT'S WHERE WE'LL GO IN FROM.
Jeremiah's plan was to rob the storefront during the rally at the Garden...
When most of their members would be at the big celebration...
And the place would, at best, have a skeleton crew on guard.
Like I said, he was smart.
THEY DO THEIR MONEY SHIPMENT EVERY WEDNESDAY...
SO ON MONDAY NIGHT, THERE SHOULD BE A LOT OF CASH IN THERE.
HOW MUCH, YOU THINK?
HARD TO SAY... HOW MUCH CAN YOU FIT INTO A WOODEN BOX?

It's strange how easily an old enemy can feel like an old friend.

But I guess neither of us had anyone left to talk to about those days...

So maybe it's not that strange.

YOU NEVER ACTUALLY CAUGHT UP WITH US *BACK THEN*, DID YOU?

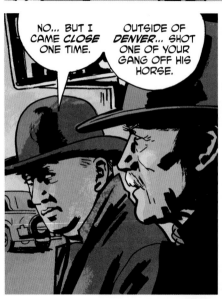

NO... BUT I CAME *CLOSE* ONE TIME.

OUTSIDE OF *DENVER*... SHOT ONE OF YOUR GANG OFF HIS HORSE.

LANNIE BARKIN.

I REMEMBER THAT.

A HELL OF A SHOT.

RIGHT THROUGH THE BACK OF HIS HEAD.

YEAH... SORRY.

DON'T BE. I *HATED* LANNIE.

HE WAS A BASTARD... ALWAYS LOOKING TO SHOOT SOMEONE...

HAD TO STOP HIM FROM RAPING A WOMAN ONE TIME.

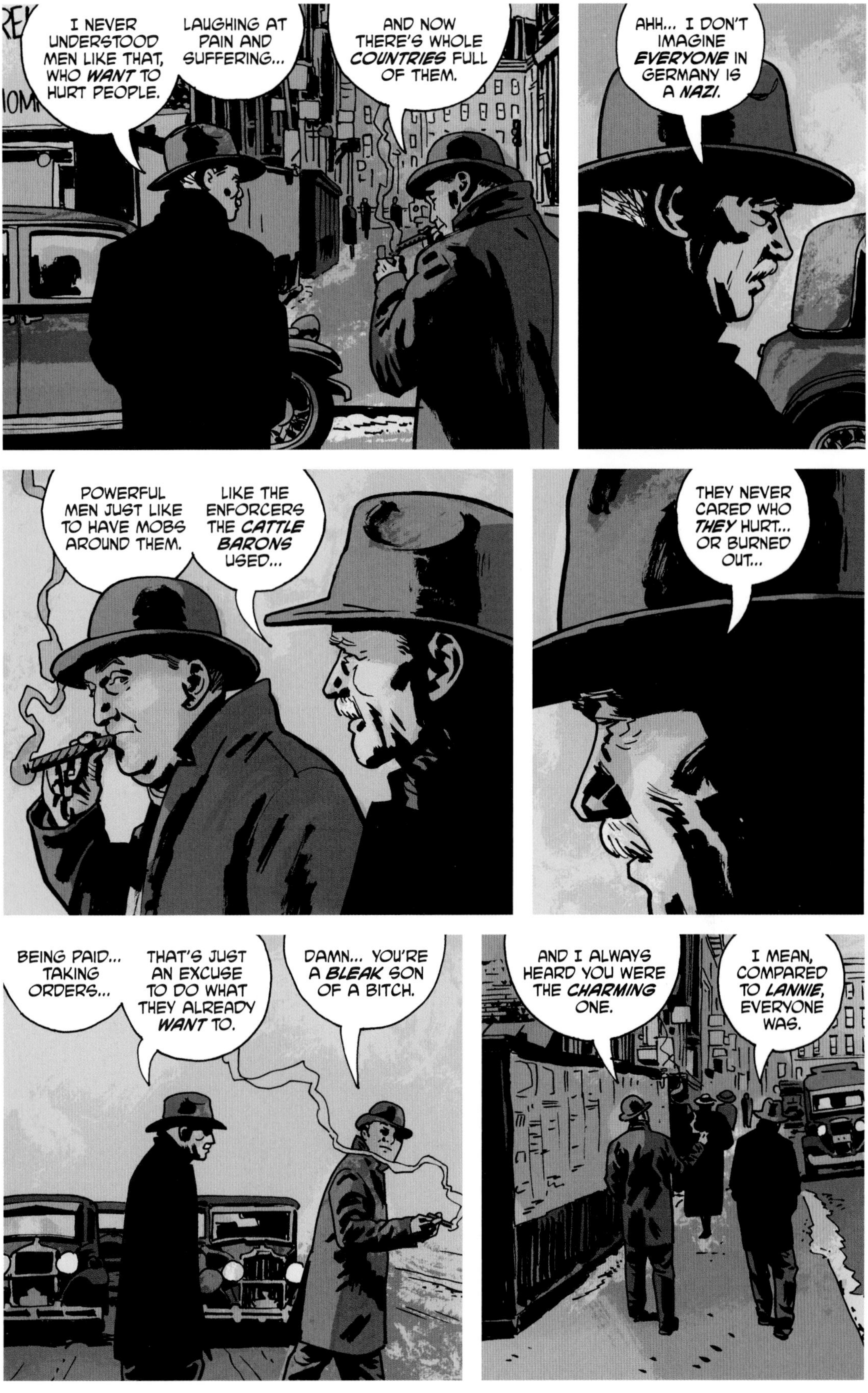
I NEVER UNDERSTOOD MEN LIKE THAT, WHO *WANT* TO HURT PEOPLE.
LAUGHING AT PAIN AND SUFFERING...
AND NOW THERE'S WHOLE *COUNTRIES* FULL OF THEM.
AHH... I DON'T IMAGINE *EVERYONE* IN GERMANY IS A *NAZI*.
POWERFUL MEN JUST LIKE TO HAVE MOBS AROUND THEM.
LIKE THE ENFORCERS THE *CATTLE BARONS* USED...
THEY NEVER CARED WHO *THEY* HURT... OR BURNED OUT...
BEING PAID... TAKING ORDERS...
THAT'S JUST AN EXCUSE TO DO WHAT THEY ALREADY *WANT* TO.
DAMN... YOU'RE A *BLEAK* SON OF A BITCH.
AND I ALWAYS HEARD YOU WERE THE *CHARMING* ONE.
I MEAN, COMPARED TO *LANNIE*, EVERYONE WAS.

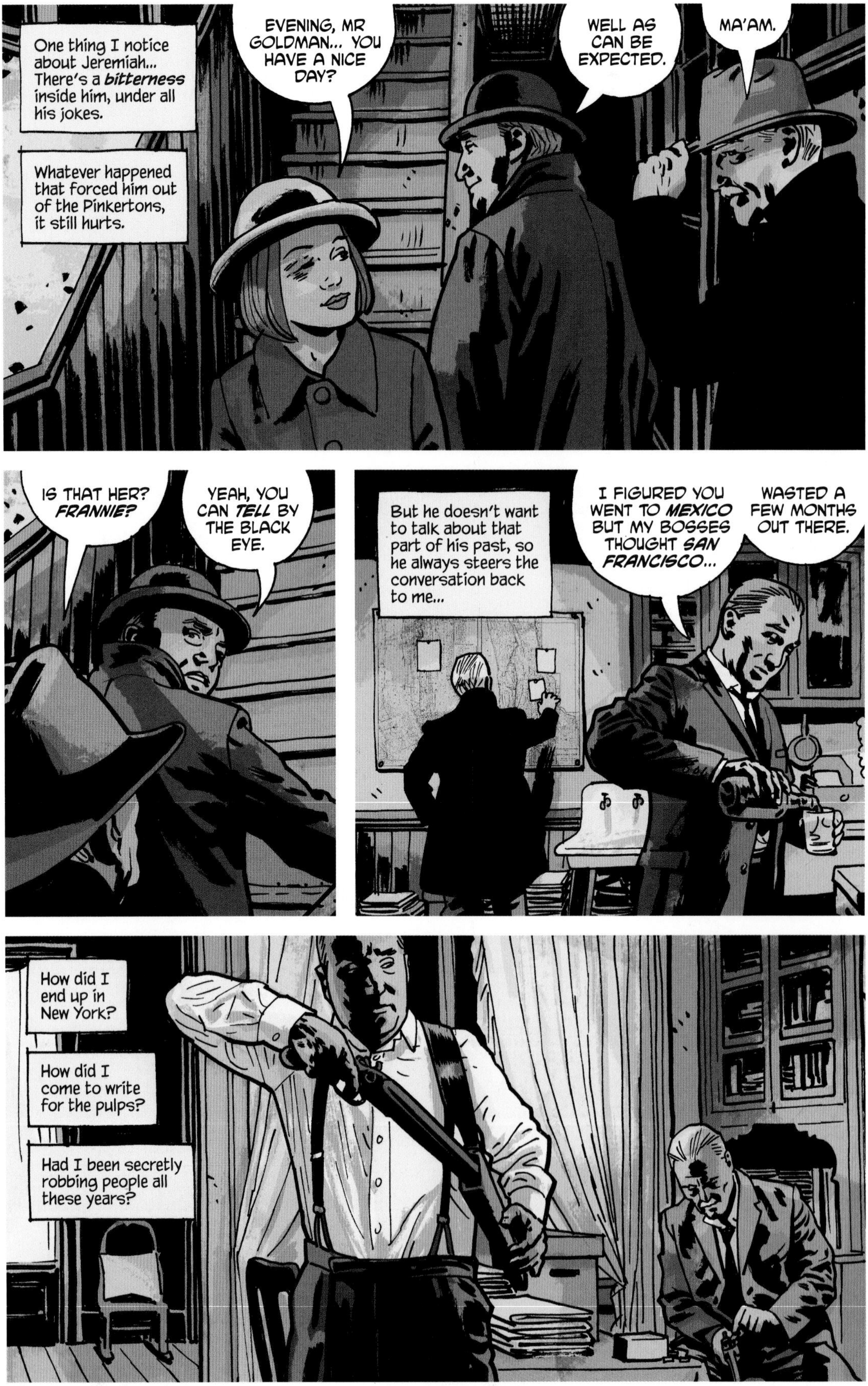
One thing I notice about Jeremiah... There's a **bitterness** inside him, under all his jokes.
Whatever happened that forced him out of the Pinkertons, it still hurts.
EVENING, MR GOLDMAN... YOU HAVE A NICE DAY?
WELL AS CAN BE EXPECTED.
MA'AM.
IS THAT HER? **FRANNIE?**
YEAH, YOU CAN **TELL** BY THE BLACK EYE.
But he doesn't want to talk about that part of his past, so he always steers the conversation back to me...
I FIGURED YOU WENT TO **MEXICO** BUT MY BOSSES THOUGHT **SAN FRANCISCO**...
WASTED A FEW MONTHS OUT THERE.
How did I end up in New York?
How did I come to write for the pulps?
Had I been secretly robbing people all these years?

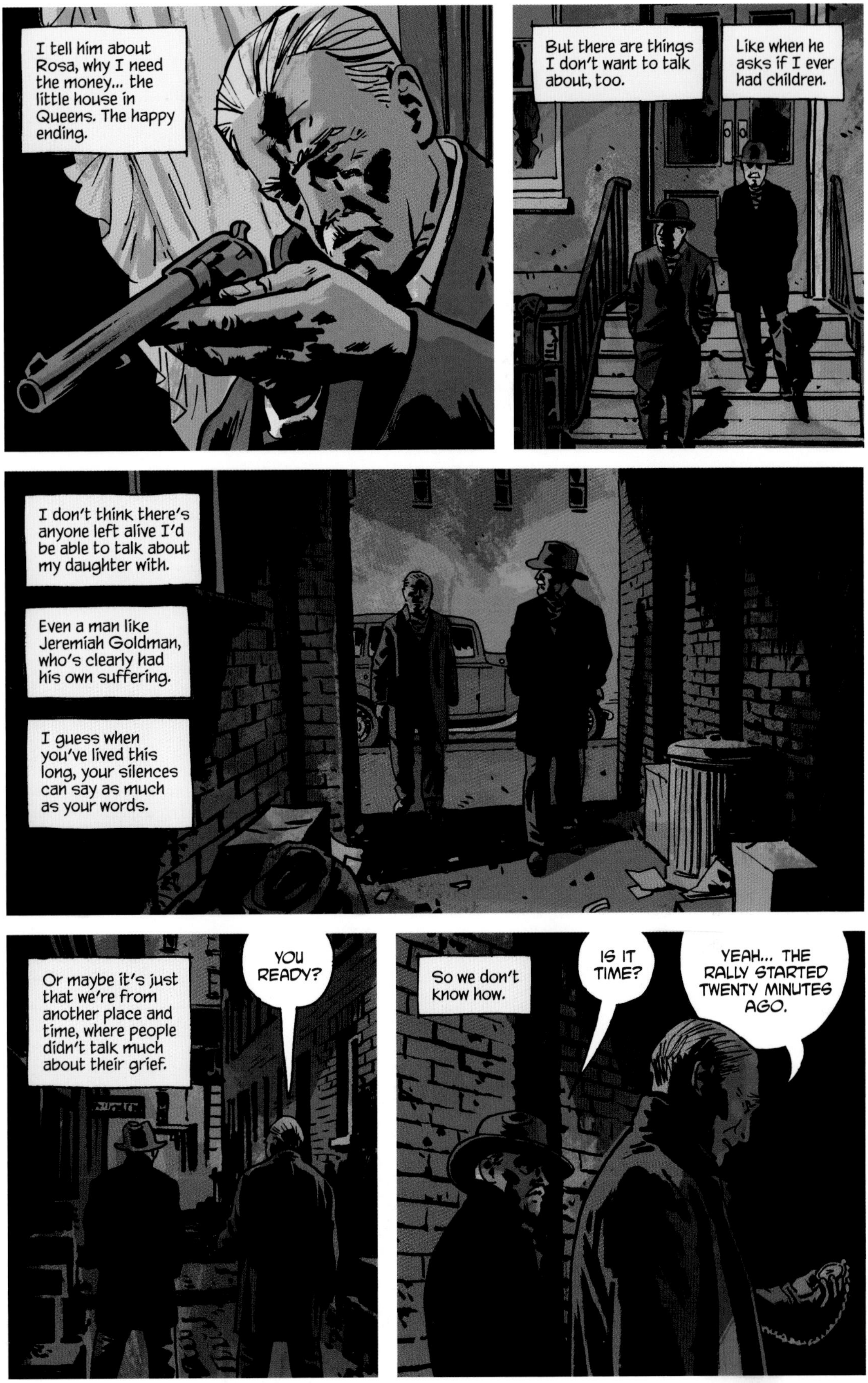
I tell him about Rosa, why I need the money... the little house in Queens. The happy ending.
But there are things I don't want to talk about, too.
Like when he asks if I ever had children.
I don't think there's anyone left alive I'd be able to talk about my daughter with.
Even a man like Jeremiah Goldman, who's clearly had his own suffering.
I guess when you've lived this long, your silences can say as much as your words.
Or maybe it's just that we're from another place and time, where people didn't talk much about their grief.
YOU READY?
So we don't know how.
IS IT TIME?
YEAH... THE RALLY STARTED TWENTY MINUTES AGO.

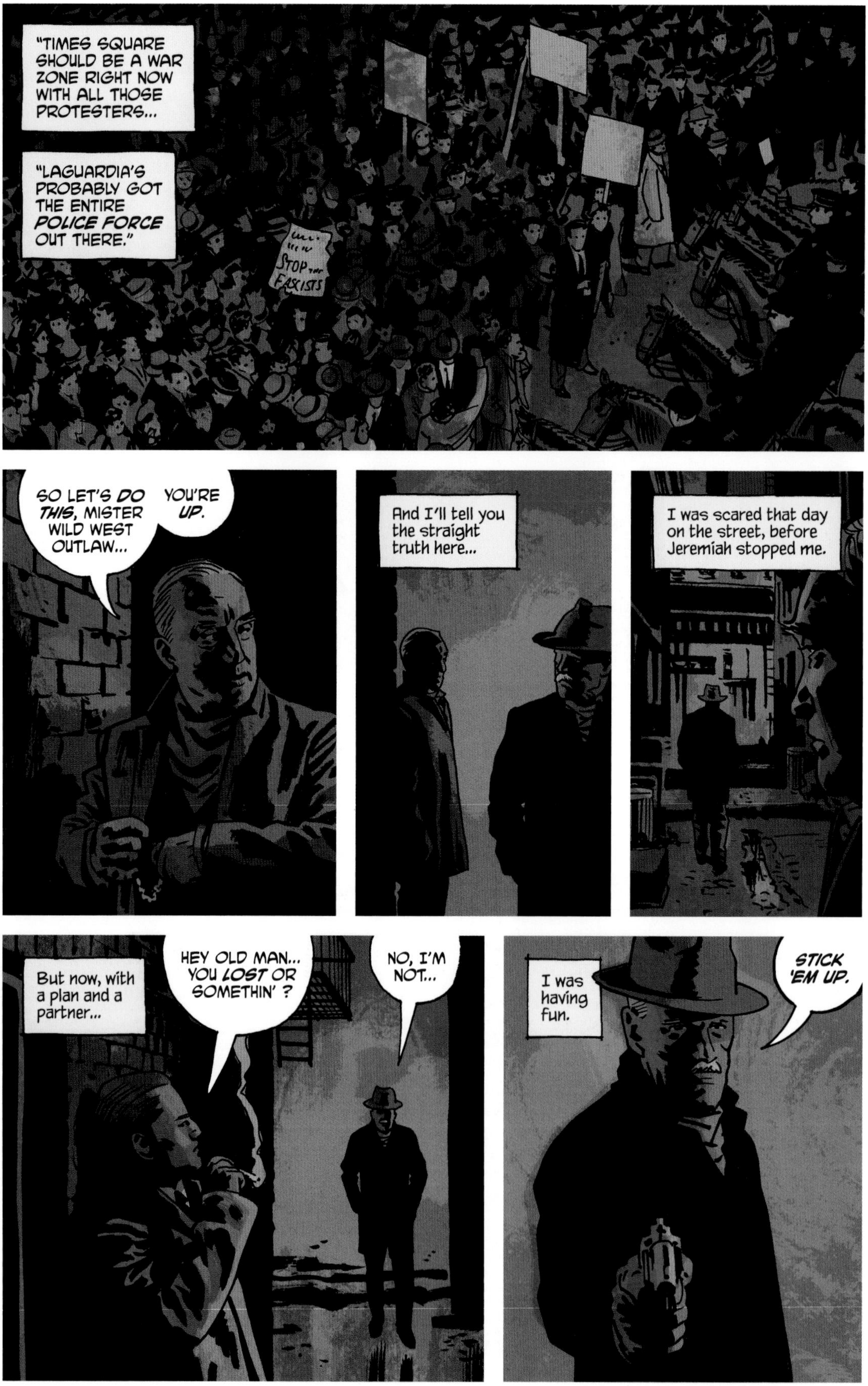
"TIMES SQUARE SHOULD BE A WAR ZONE RIGHT NOW WITH ALL THOSE PROTESTERS...
"LAGUARDIA'S PROBABLY GOT THE ENTIRE *POLICE FORCE* OUT THERE."
STOP
FASCISTS
SO LET'S *DO THIS*, MISTER WILD WEST OUTLAW...
YOU'RE *UP*.
And I'll tell you the straight truth here...
I was scared that day on the street, before Jeremiah stopped me.
But now, with a plan and a partner...
HEY OLD MAN... YOU *LOST* OR SOMETHIN' ?
NO, I'M NOT...
I was having fun.
STICK 'EM UP.

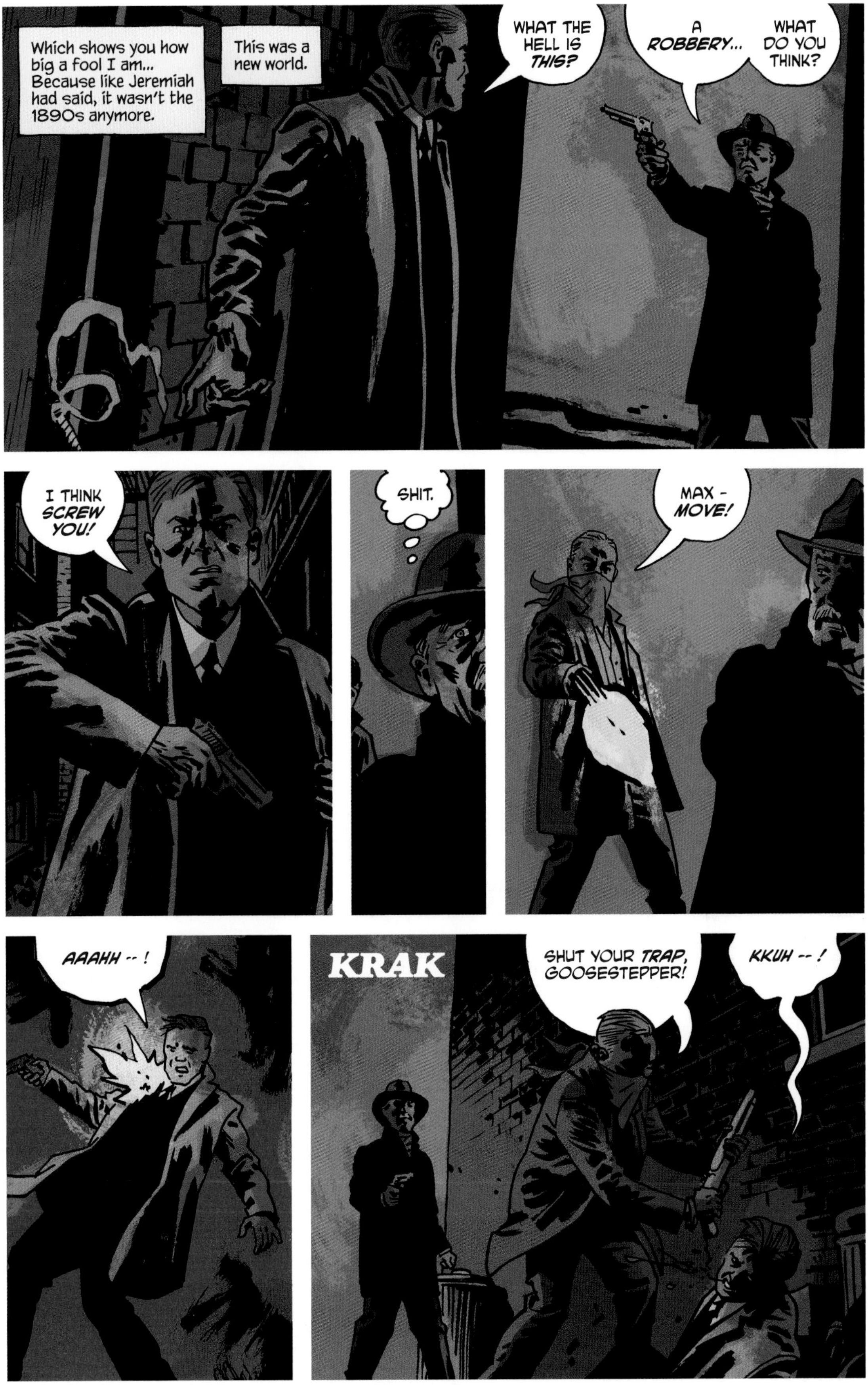
Which shows you how big a fool I am... Because like Jeremiah had said, it wasn't the 1890s anymore.
This was a new world.
WHAT THE HELL IS *THIS?*
A *ROBBERY*...
WHAT DO YOU THINK?
I THINK *SCREW YOU!*
SHIT.
MAX - *MOVE!*
AAAHH -- !
KRAK
SHUT YOUR *TRAP*, GOOSESTEPPER!
KKUH -- !

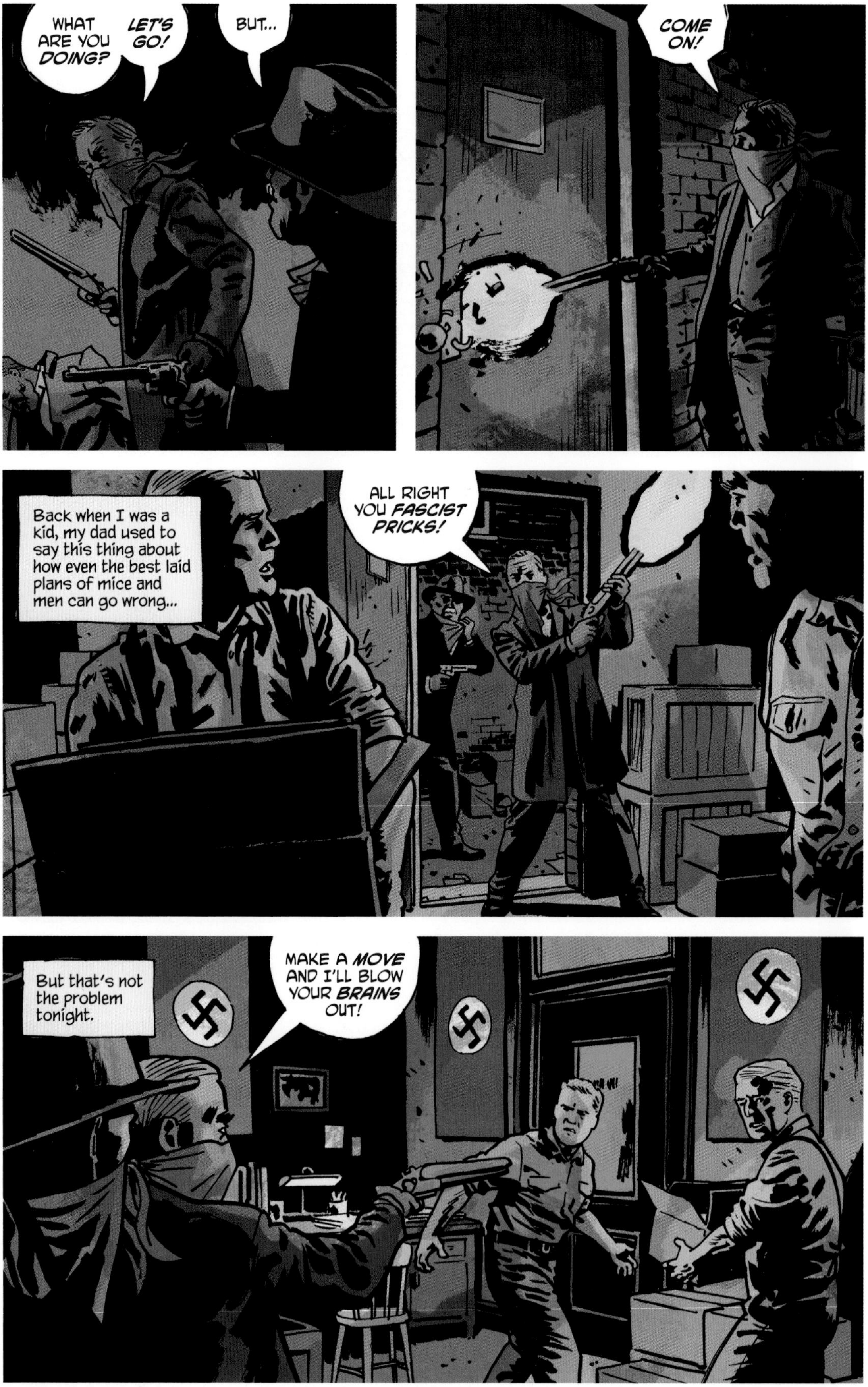
WHAT ARE YOU *DOING?*
LET'S GO!
BUT...
COME ON!
Back when I was a kid, my dad used to say this thing about how even the best laid plans of mice and men can go wrong...
ALL RIGHT YOU *FASCIST PRICKS!*
But that's not the problem tonight.
MAKE A *MOVE* AND I'LL BLOW YOUR *BRAINS* OUT!

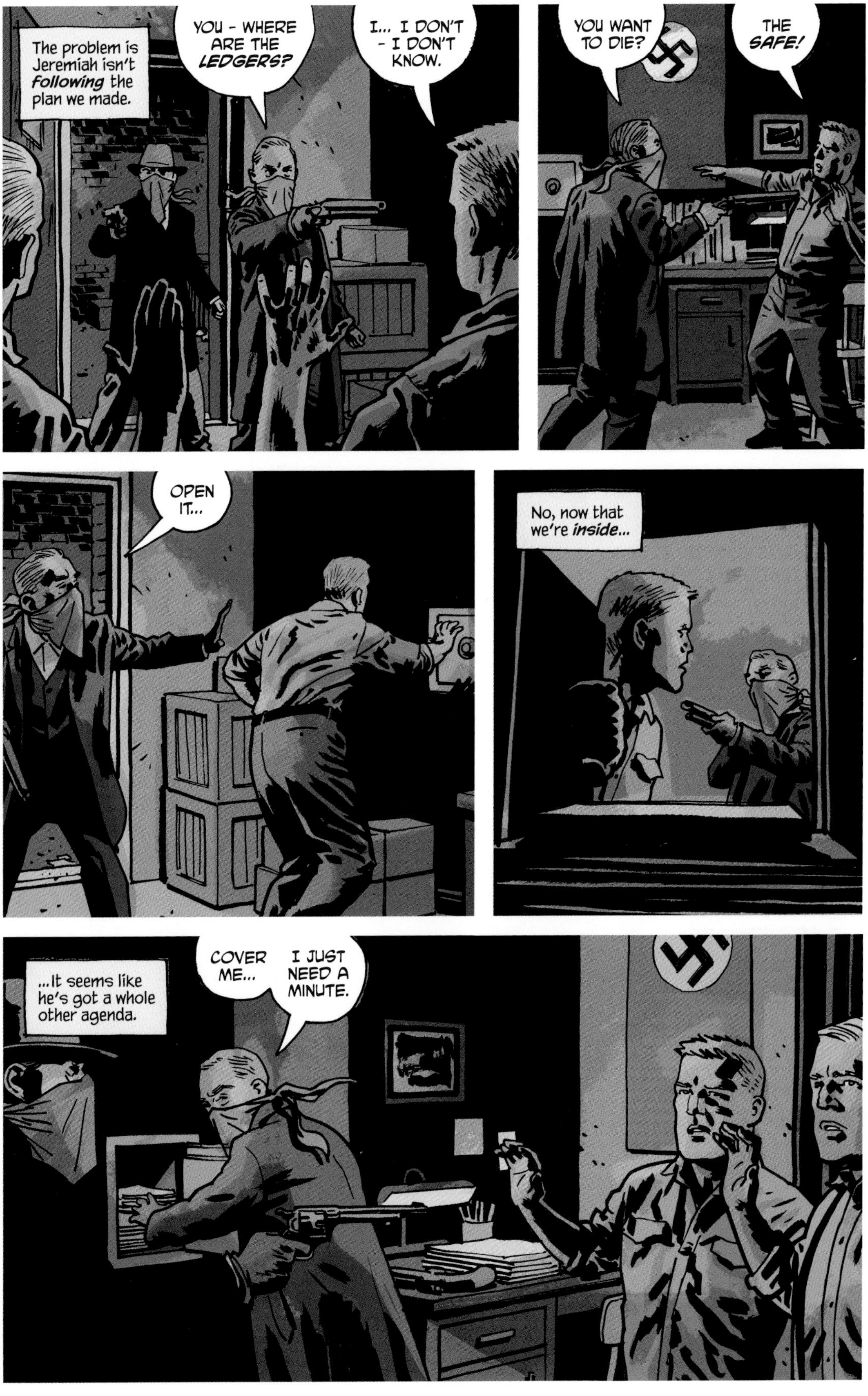
The problem is Jeremiah isn't *following* the plan we made.
YOU - WHERE ARE THE *LEDGERS?*
I... I DON'T - I DON'T KNOW.
YOU WANT TO DIE?
THE *SAFE!*
OPEN IT...
No, now that we're *inside*...
...It seems like he's got a whole other agenda.
COVER ME...
I JUST NEED A MINUTE.

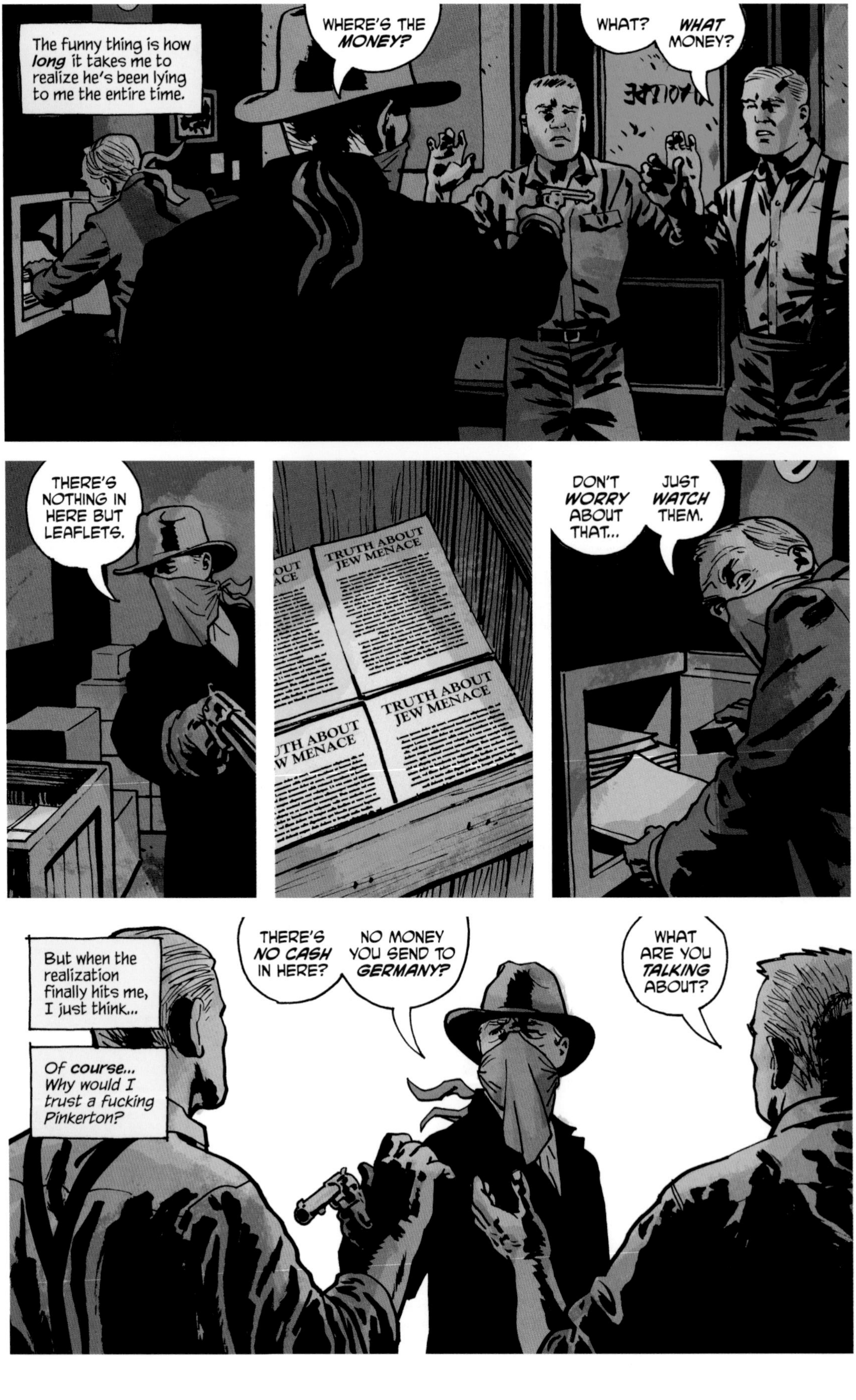

The funny thing is how long it takes me to realize he's been lying to me the entire time.
WHERE'S THE MONEY?
WHAT?
WHAT MONEY?
THERE'S NOTHING IN HERE BUT LEAFLETS.
TRUTH ABOUT JEW MENACE
TRUTH ABOUT JEW MENACE
DON'T WORRY ABOUT THAT...
JUST WATCH THEM.
But when the realization finally hits me, I just think...
Of course... Why would I trust a fucking Pinkerton?
THERE'S NO CASH IN HERE?
NO MONEY YOU SEND TO GERMANY?
WHAT ARE YOU TALKING ABOUT?

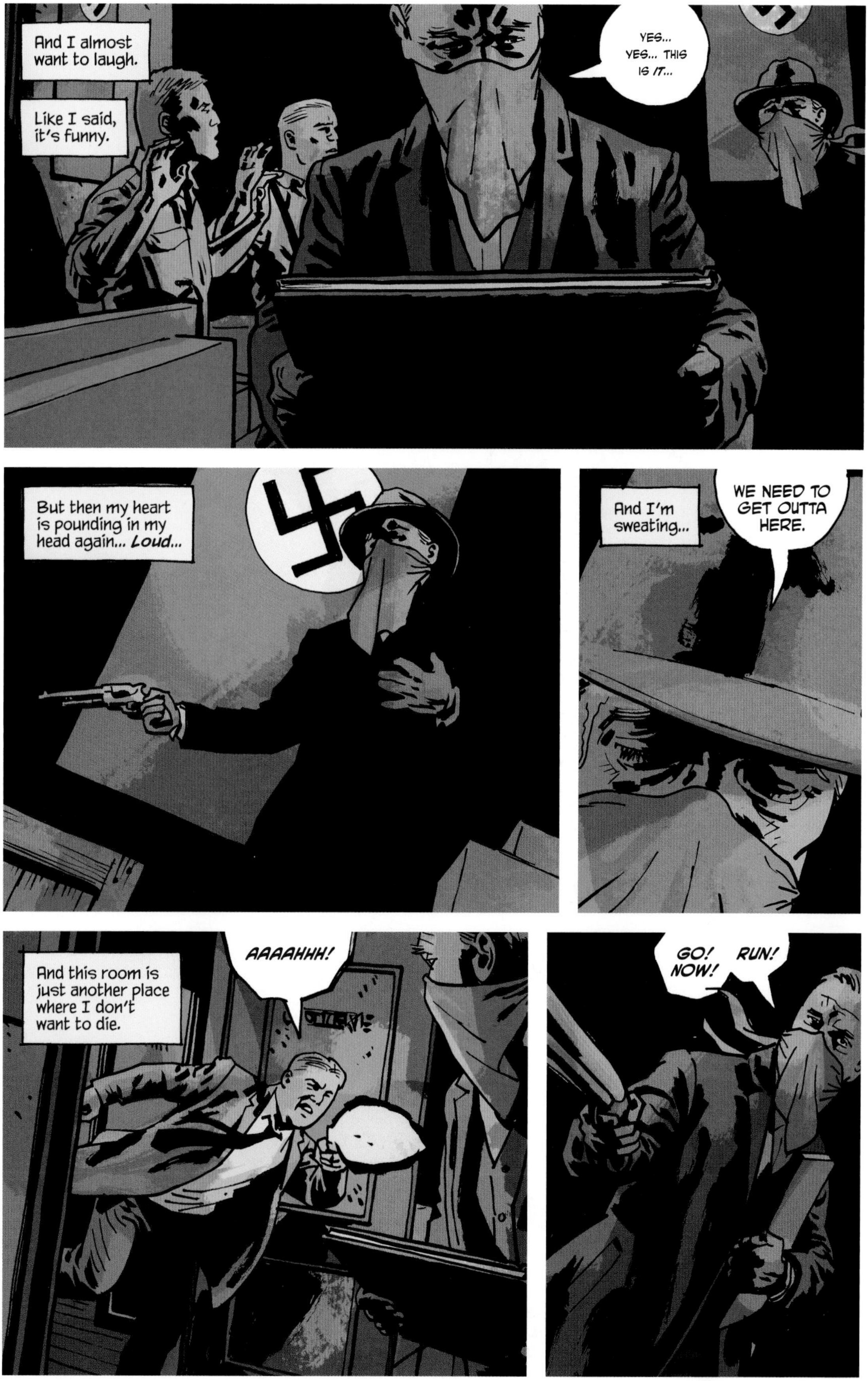
And I almost want to laugh.
Like I said, it's funny.
YES... YES... THIS IS IT...
But then my heart is pounding in my head again... Loud...
And I'm sweating...
WE NEED TO GET OUTTA HERE.
And this room is just another place where I don't want to die.
AAAAHHH!
GO! NOW!
RUN!

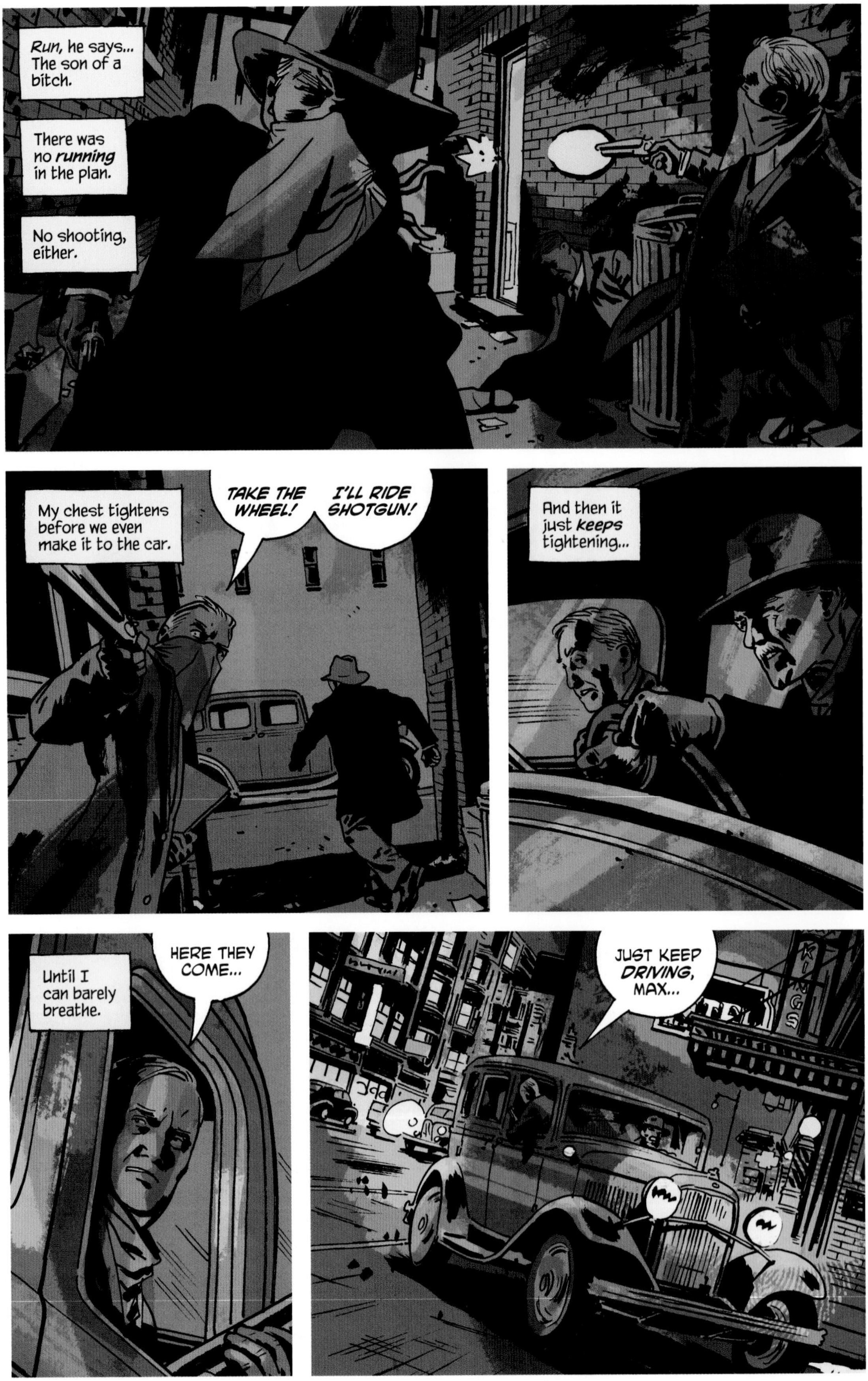
Run, he says... The son of a bitch.
There was no ***running*** in the plan.
No shooting, either.
My chest tightens before we even make it to the car.
TAKE THE WHEEL!
I'LL RIDE SHOTGUN!
And then it just ***keeps*** tightening...
Until I can barely breathe.
HERE THEY COME...
JUST KEEP *DRIVING,* MAX...

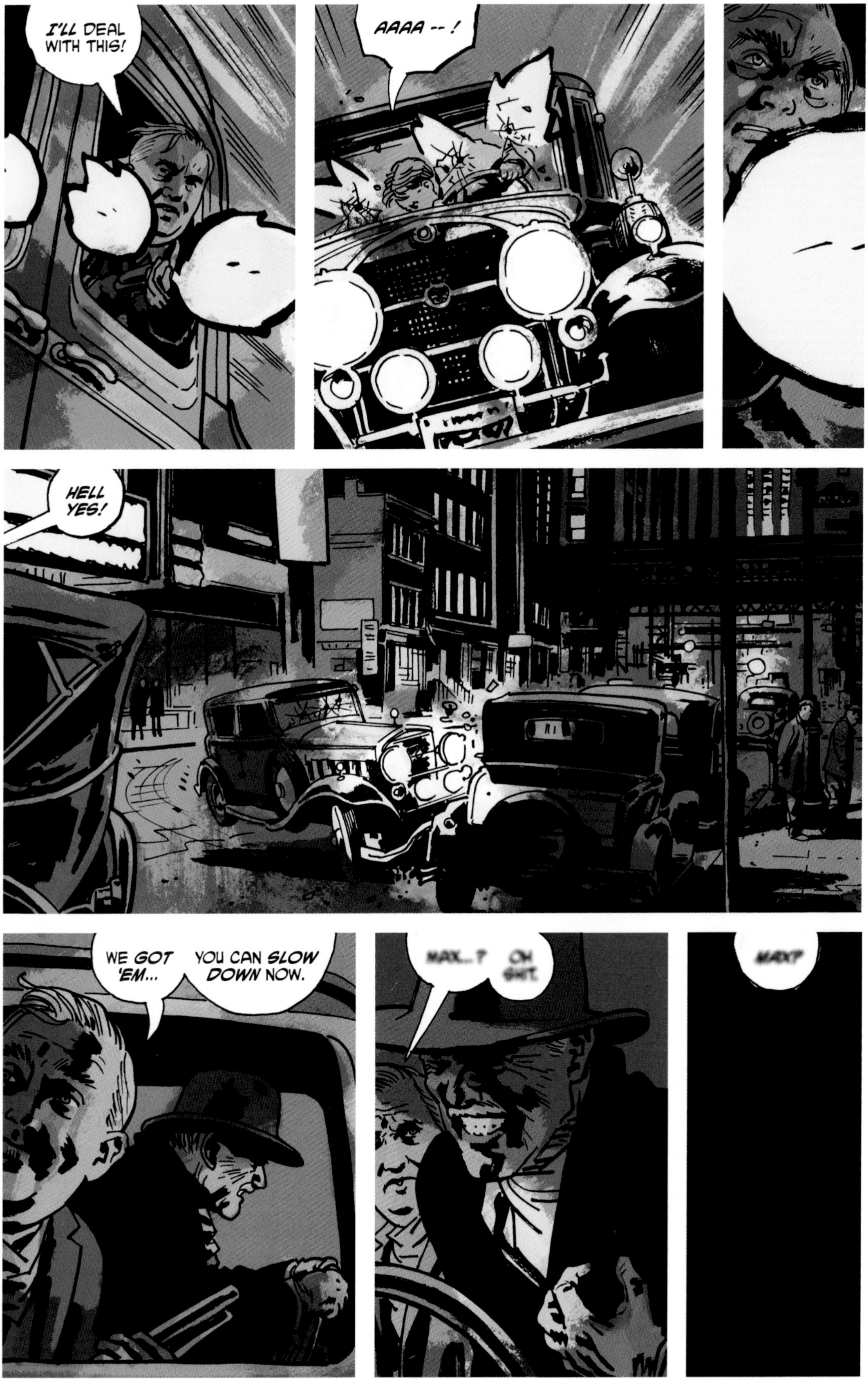
I'LL DEAL WITH THIS!
AAAA -- !
HELL YES!
WE GOT 'EM...
YOU CAN SLOW DOWN NOW.
MAX...?
OH SHIT.
MAX?

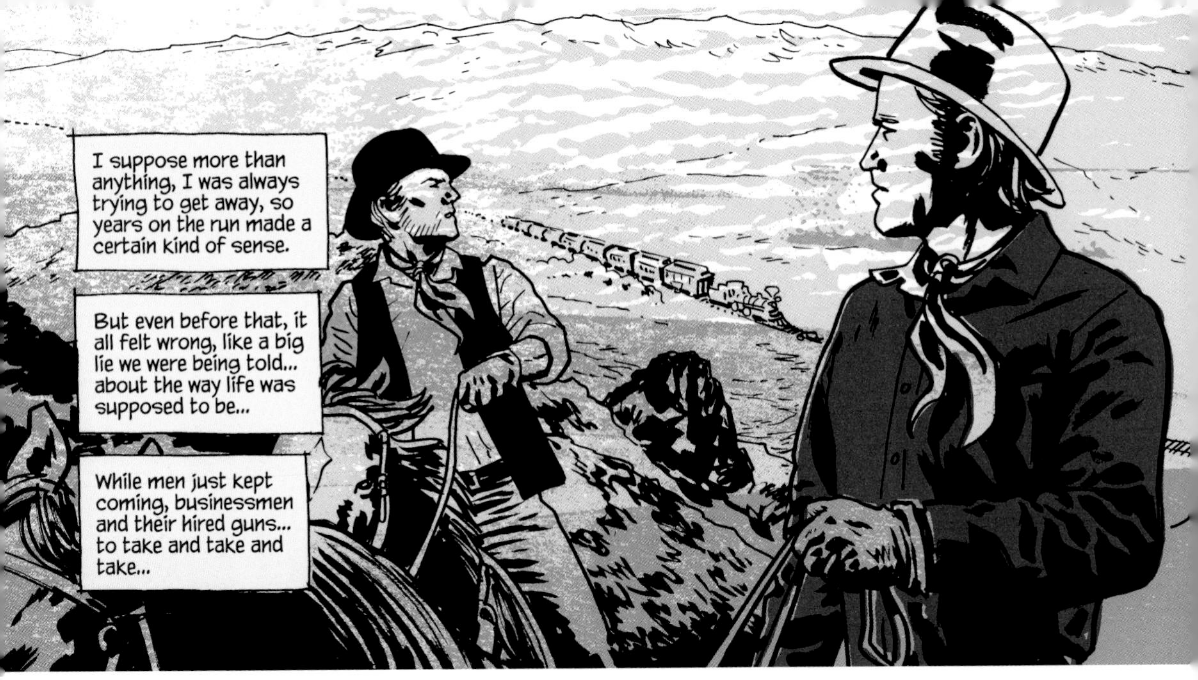
I suppose more than anything, I was always trying to get away, so years on the run made a certain kind of sense.
But even before that, it all felt wrong, like a big lie we were being told... about the way life was supposed to be...
While men just kept coming, businessmen and their hired guns... to take and take and take...

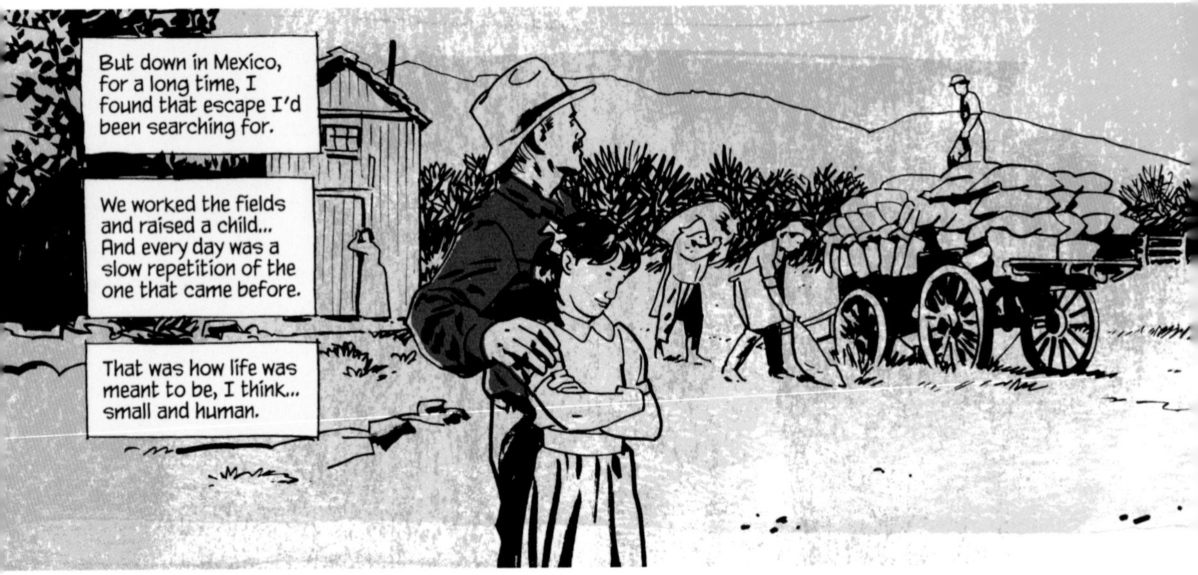
But down in Mexico, for a long time, I found that escape I'd been searching for.
We worked the fields and raised a child... And every day was a slow repetition of the one that came before.
That was how life was meant to be, I think... small and human.

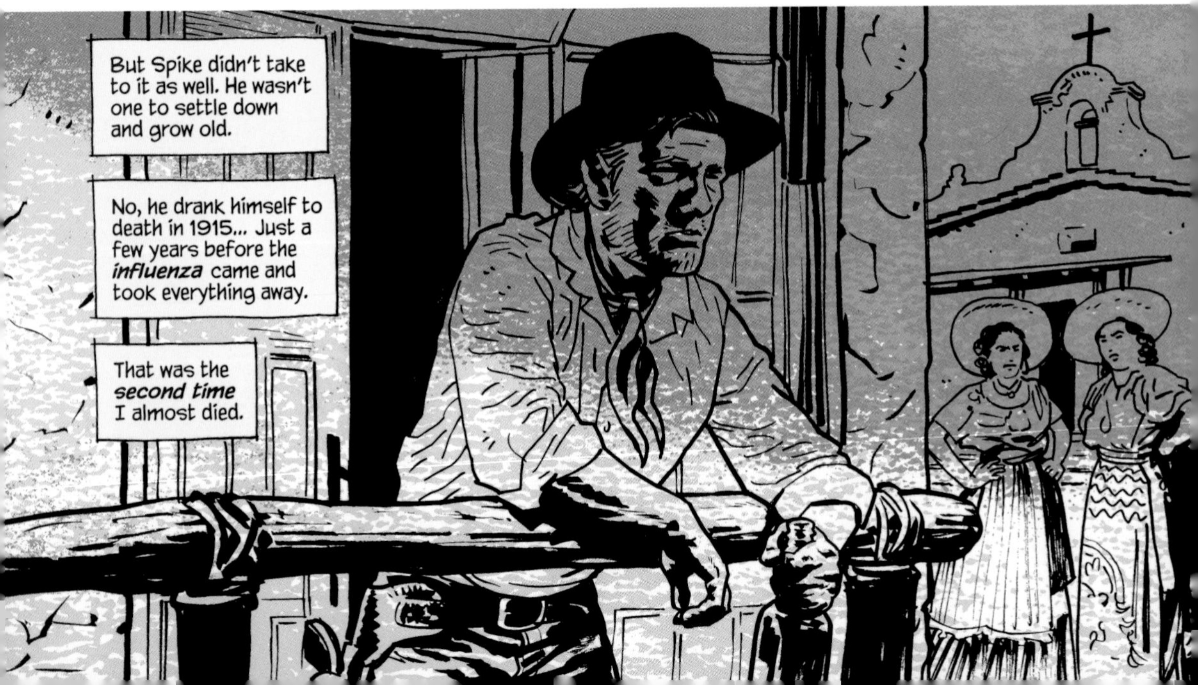
But Spike didn't take to it as well. He wasn't one to settle down and grow old.
No, he drank himself to death in 1915... Just a few years before the *influenza* came and took everything away.
That was the *second time* I almost died.

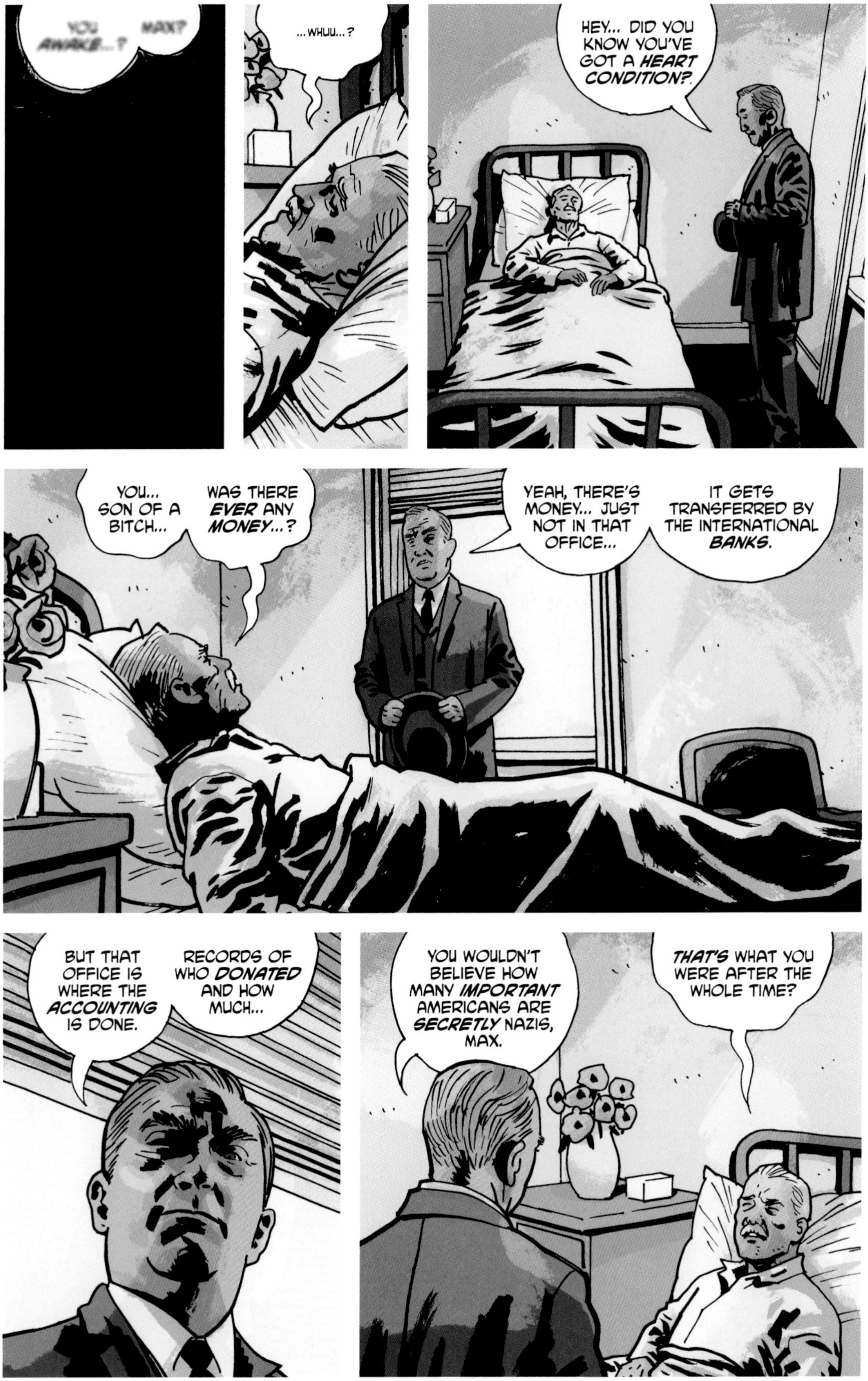
YOU AWAKE...?
MAX?
...WHUU...?
HEY... DID YOU KNOW YOU'VE GOT A HEART CONDITION?
YOU... SON OF A BITCH...
WAS THERE EVER ANY MONEY...?
YEAH, THERE'S MONEY... JUST NOT IN THAT OFFICE...
IT GETS TRANSFERRED BY THE INTERNATIONAL BANKS.
BUT THAT OFFICE IS WHERE THE ACCOUNTING IS DONE.
RECORDS OF WHO DONATED AND HOW MUCH...
YOU WOULDN'T BELIEVE HOW MANY IMPORTANT AMERICANS ARE SECRETLY NAZIS, MAX.
THAT'S WHAT YOU WERE AFTER THE WHOLE TIME?

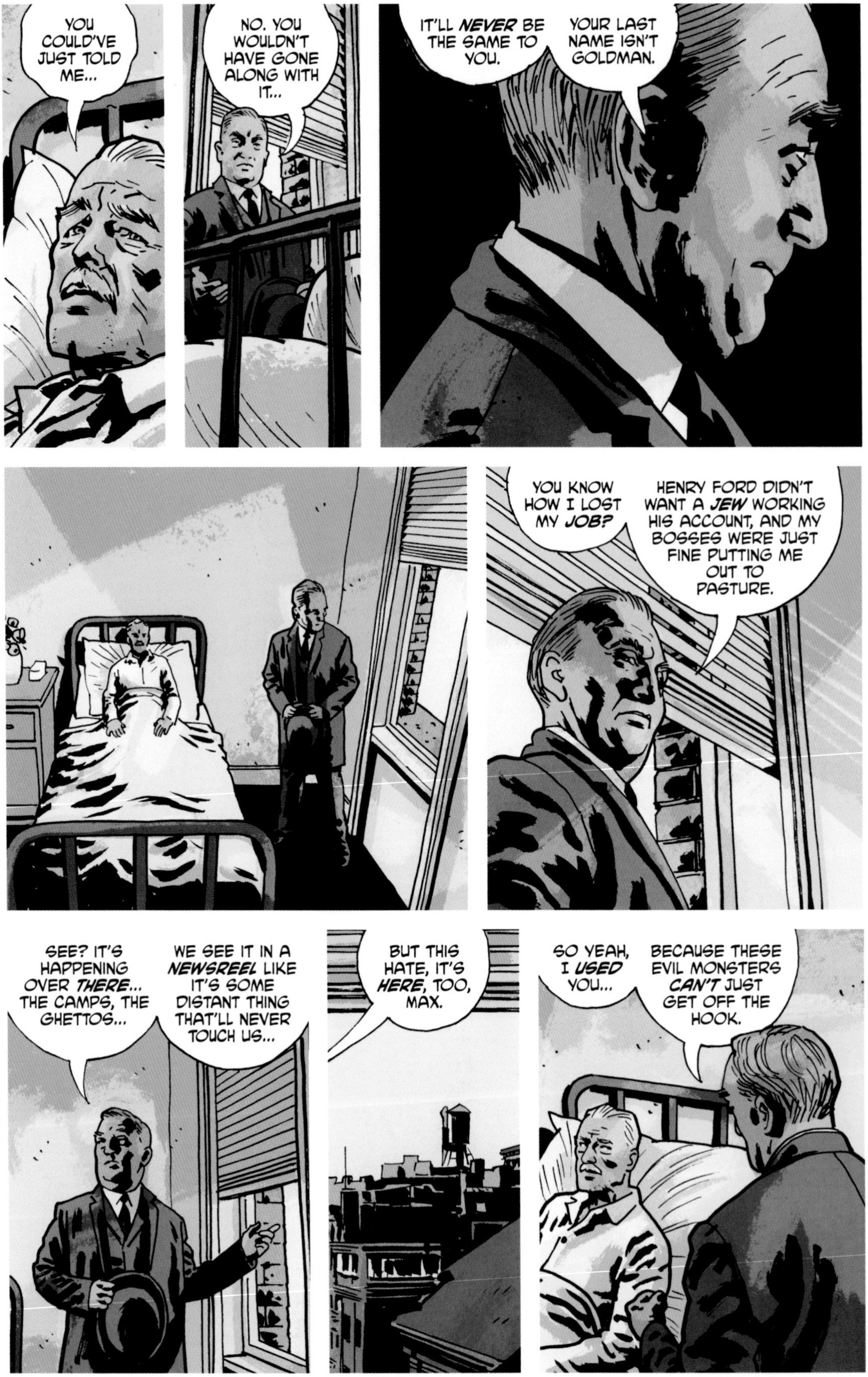
YOU COULD'VE JUST TOLD ME...
NO. YOU WOULDN'T HAVE GONE ALONG WITH IT...
IT'LL NEVER BE THE SAME TO YOU.
YOUR LAST NAME ISN'T GOLDMAN.
YOU KNOW HOW I LOST MY JOB?
HENRY FORD DIDN'T WANT A JEW WORKING HIS ACCOUNT, AND MY BOSSES WERE JUST FINE PUTTING ME OUT TO PASTURE.
SEE? IT'S HAPPENING OVER THERE... THE CAMPS, THE GHETTOS...
WE SEE IT IN A NEWSREEL LIKE IT'S SOME DISTANT THING THAT'LL NEVER TOUCH US...
BUT THIS HATE, IT'S HERE, TOO, MAX.
SO YEAH, I USED YOU...
BECAUSE THESE EVIL MONSTERS CAN'T JUST GET OFF THE HOOK.

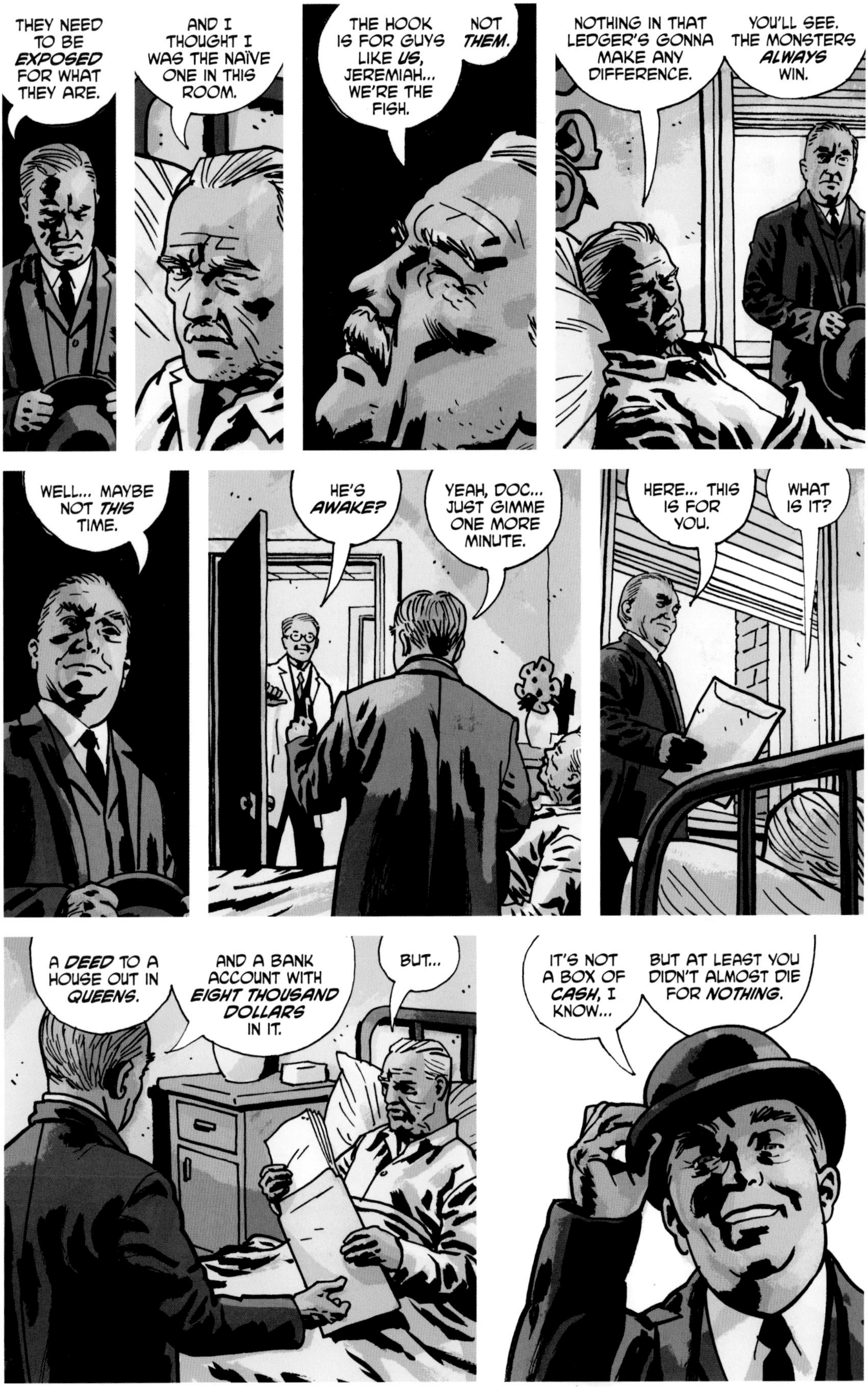
THEY NEED TO BE EXPOSED FOR WHAT THEY ARE.
AND I THOUGHT I WAS THE NAÏVE ONE IN THIS ROOM.
THE HOOK IS FOR GUYS LIKE US, JEREMIAH... WE'RE THE FISH.
NOT THEM.
NOTHING IN THAT LEDGER'S GONNA MAKE ANY DIFFERENCE.
YOU'LL SEE. THE MONSTERS ALWAYS WIN.
WELL... MAYBE NOT THIS TIME.
HE'S AWAKE?
YEAH, DOC... JUST GIMME ONE MORE MINUTE.
HERE... THIS IS FOR YOU.
WHAT IS IT?
A DEED TO A HOUSE OUT IN QUEENS.
AND A BANK ACCOUNT WITH EIGHT THOUSAND DOLLARS IN IT.
BUT...
IT'S NOT A BOX OF CASH, I KNOW...
BUT AT LEAST YOU DIDN'T ALMOST DIE FOR NOTHING.

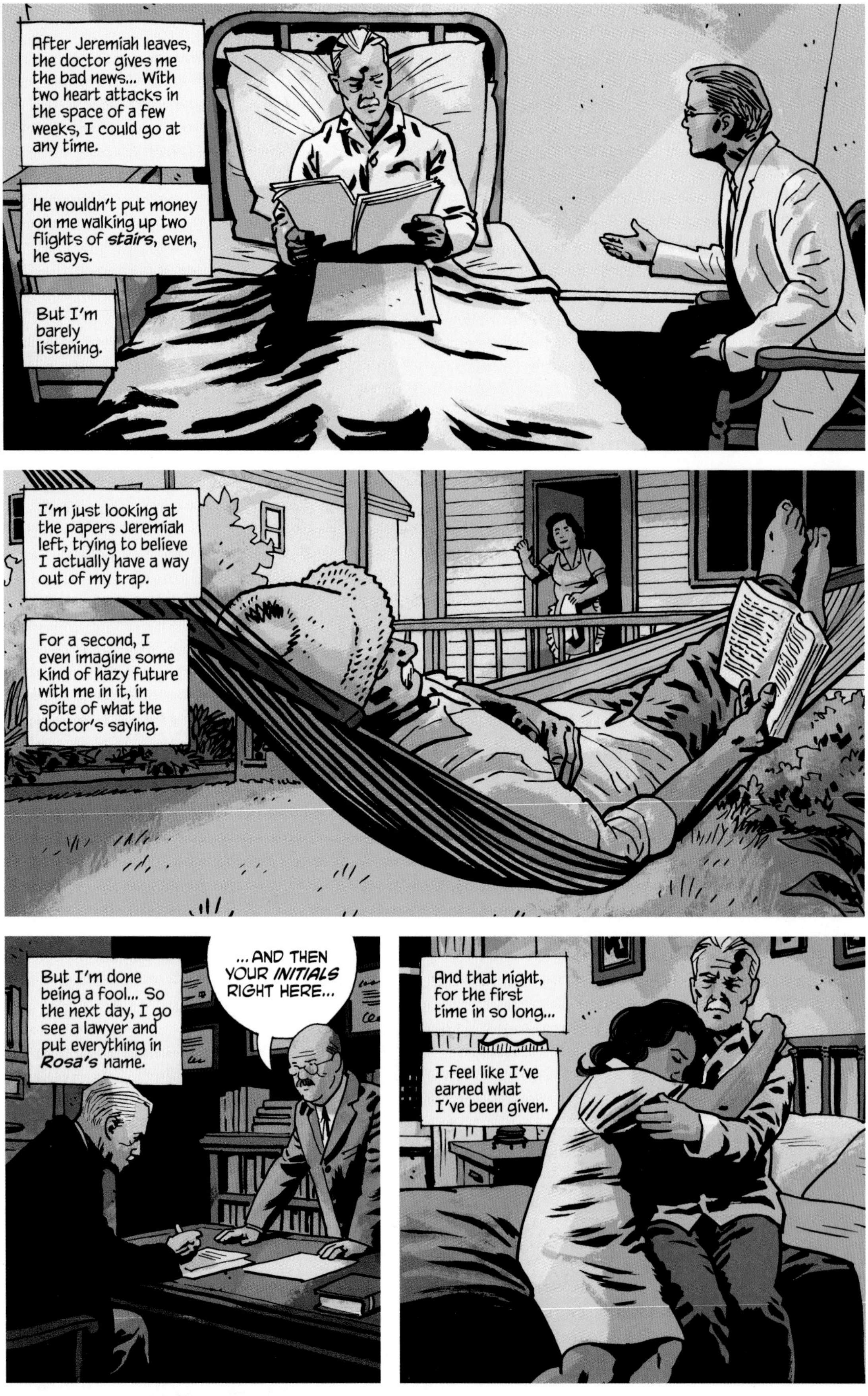

After Jeremiah leaves, the doctor gives me the bad news... With two heart attacks in the space of a few weeks, I could go at any time.
He wouldn't put money on me walking up two flights of *stairs*, even, he says.
But I'm barely listening.
I'm just looking at the papers Jeremiah left, trying to believe I actually have a way out of my trap.
For a second, I even imagine some kind of hazy future with me in it, in spite of what the doctor's saying.
But I'm done being a fool... So the next day, I go see a lawyer and put everything in *Rosa's* name.
...AND THEN YOUR *INITIALS* RIGHT HERE...
And that night, for the first time in so long...
I feel like I've earned what I've been given.

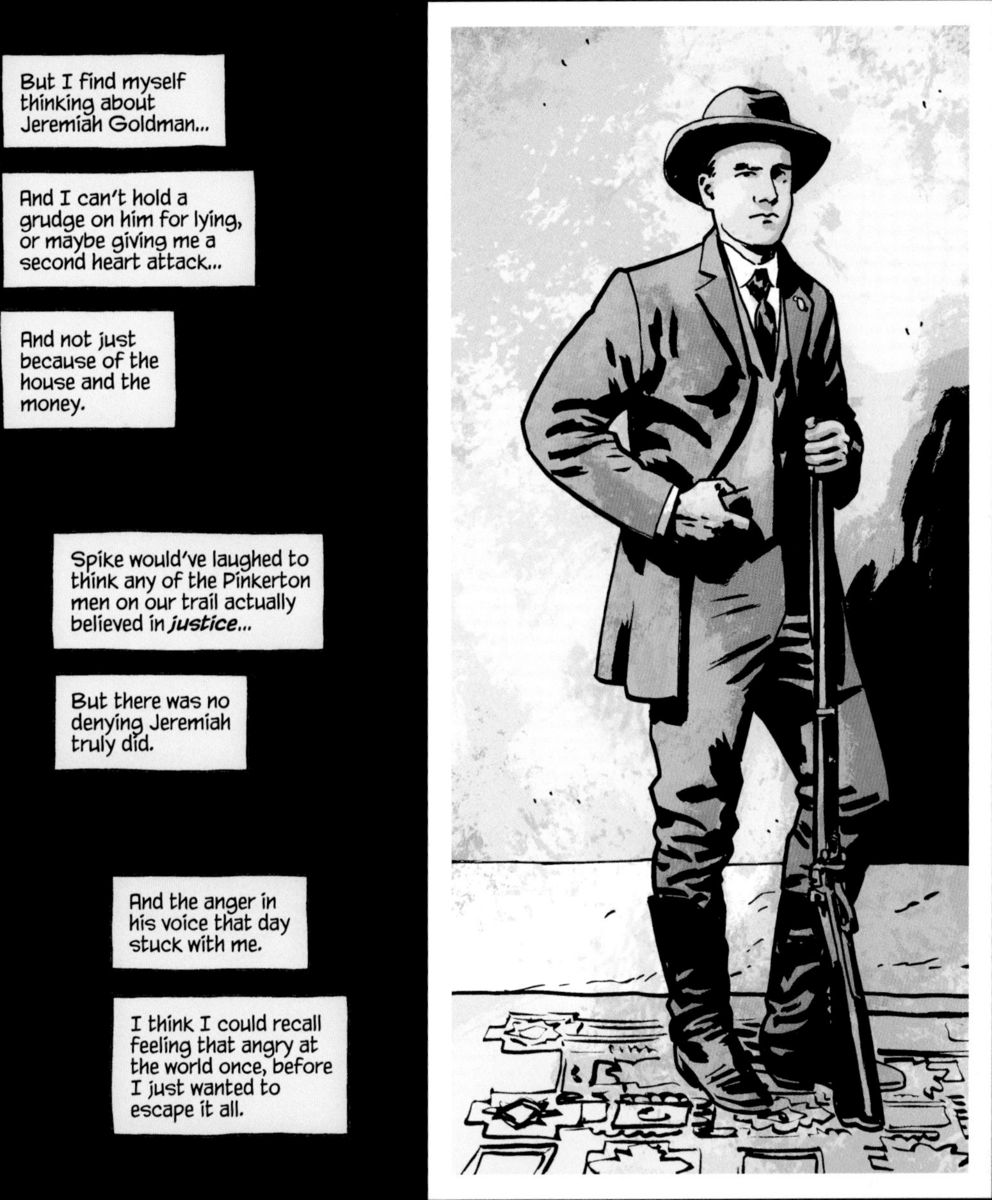
But I find myself thinking about Jeremiah Goldman...
And I can't hold a grudge on him for lying, or maybe giving me a second heart attack...
And not just because of the house and the money.
Spike would've laughed to think any of the Pinkerton men on our trail actually believed in *justice*...
But there was no denying Jeremiah truly did.
And the anger in his voice that day stuck with me.
I think I could recall feeling that angry at the world once, before I just wanted to escape it all.

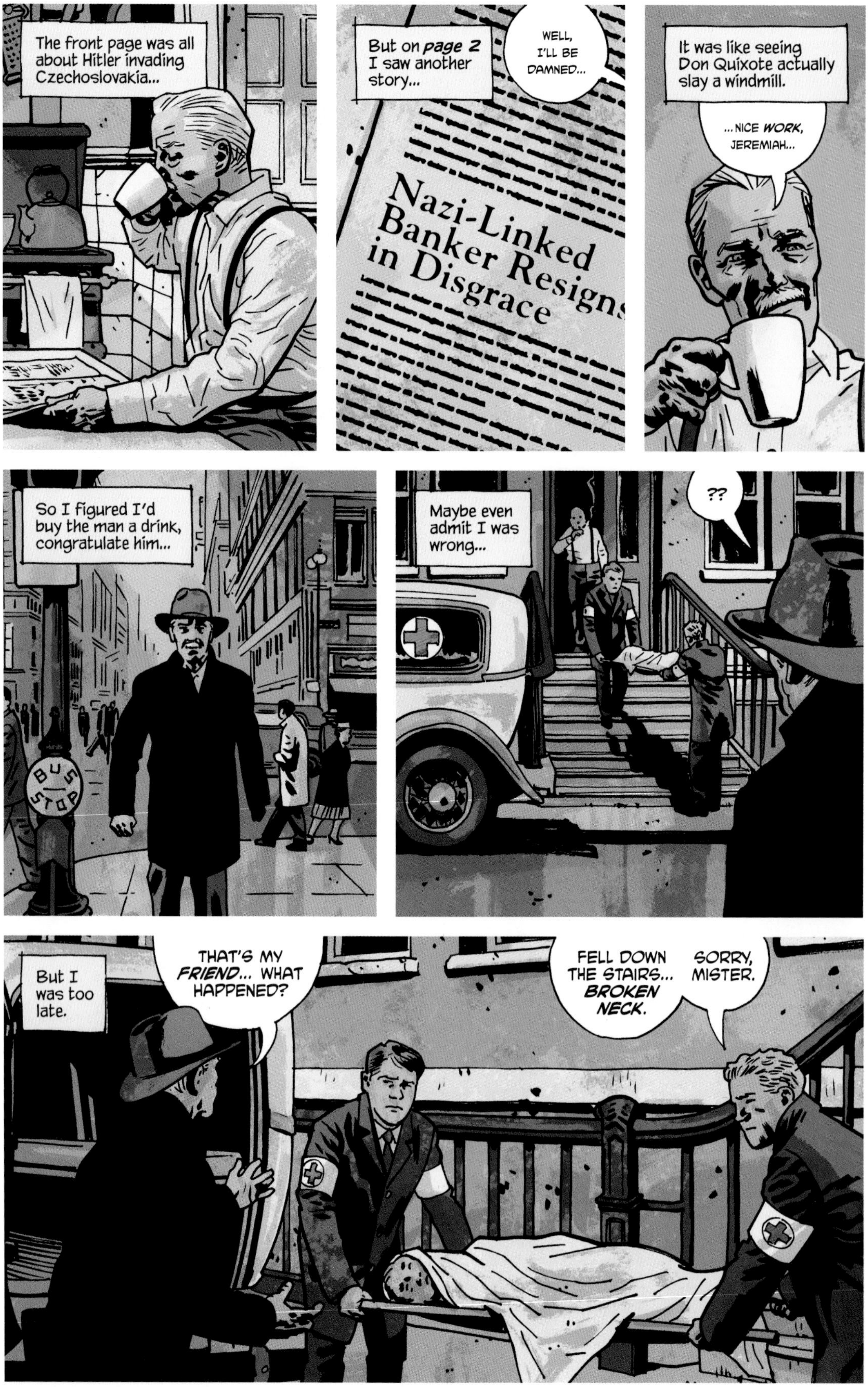
The front page was all about Hitler invading Czechoslovakia...
But on page 2 I saw another story...
WELL, I'LL BE DAMNED...
Nazi-Linked Banker Resigns in Disgrace
It was like seeing Don Quixote actually slay a windmill.
...NICE WORK, JEREMIAH...
So I figured I'd buy the man a drink, congratulate him...
BUS STOP
Maybe even admit I was wrong...
??
But I was too late.
THAT'S MY FRIEND... WHAT HAPPENED?
FELL DOWN THE STAIRS... BROKEN NECK.
SORRY, MISTER.

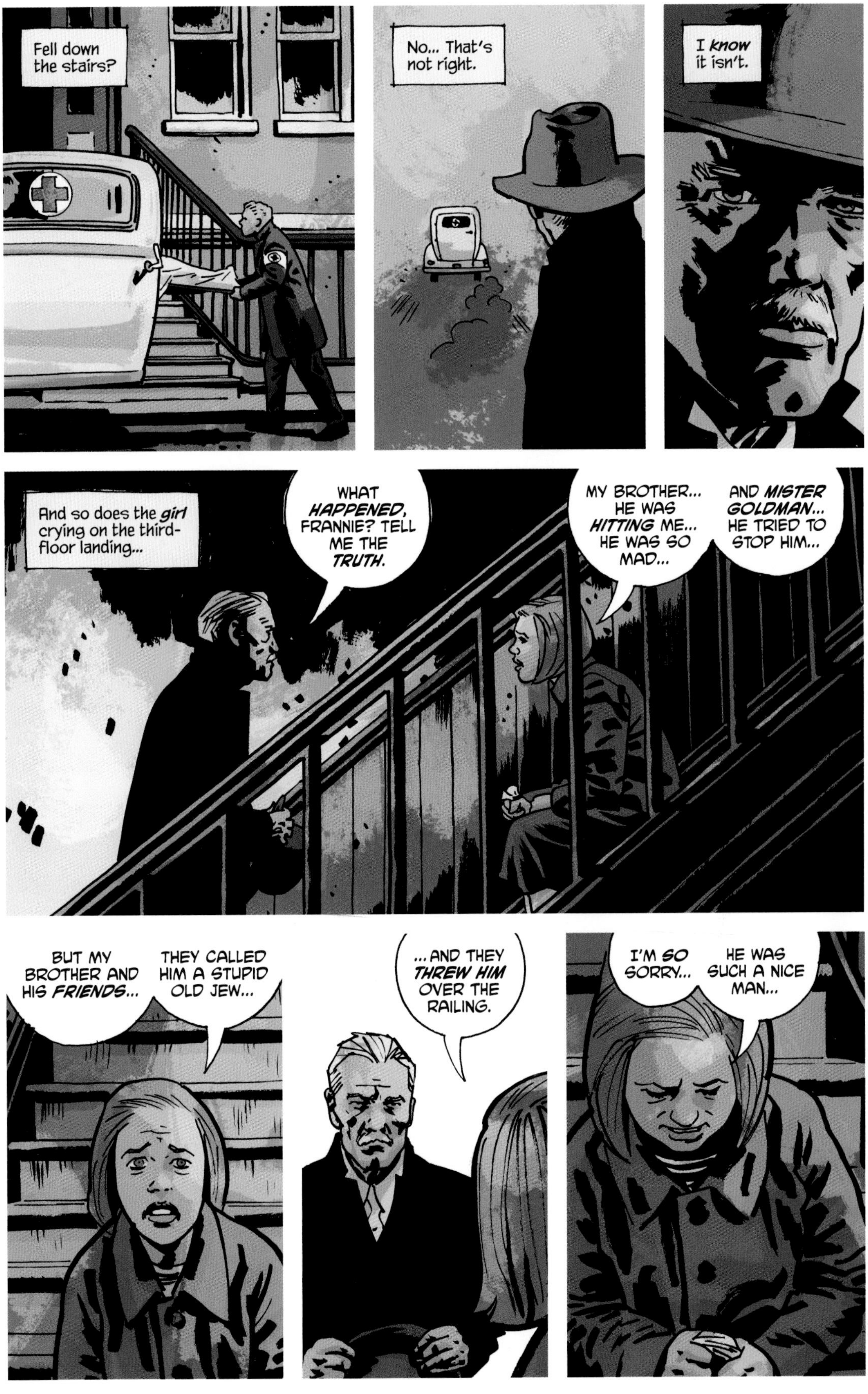
Fell down the stairs?
No... That's not right.
I *know* it isn't.
And so does the *girl* crying on the third-floor landing...
WHAT *HAPPENED,* FRANNIE? TELL ME THE *TRUTH.*
MY BROTHER... HE WAS *HITTING* ME... HE WAS SO MAD...
AND *MISTER GOLDMAN*... HE TRIED TO STOP HIM...
BUT MY BROTHER AND HIS *FRIENDS*...
THEY CALLED HIM A STUPID OLD JEW...
...AND THEY *THREW HIM* OVER THE RAILING.
I'M *SO* SORRY...
HE WAS SUCH A NICE MAN...

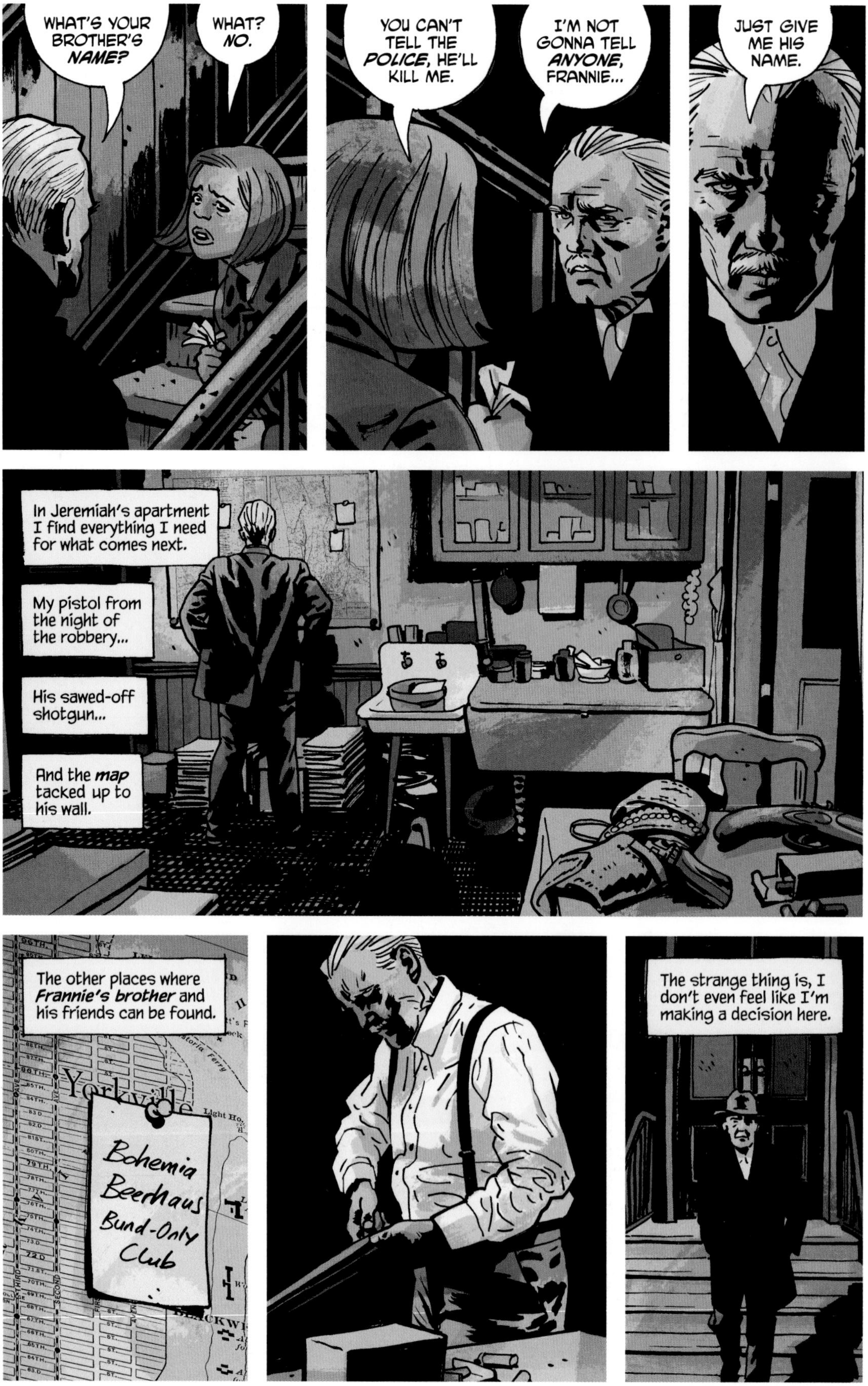
WHAT'S YOUR BROTHER'S *NAME?*
WHAT? *NO.*
YOU CAN'T TELL THE *POLICE*, HE'LL KILL ME.
I'M NOT GONNA TELL *ANYONE*, FRANNIE...
JUST GIVE ME HIS NAME.
In Jeremiah's apartment I find everything I need for what comes next.
My pistol from the night of the robbery...
His sawed-off shotgun...
And the *map* tacked up to his wall.
The other places where *Frannie's brother* and his friends can be found.
Bohemia Beerhaus Bund-Only Club
The strange thing is, I don't even feel like I'm making a decision here.

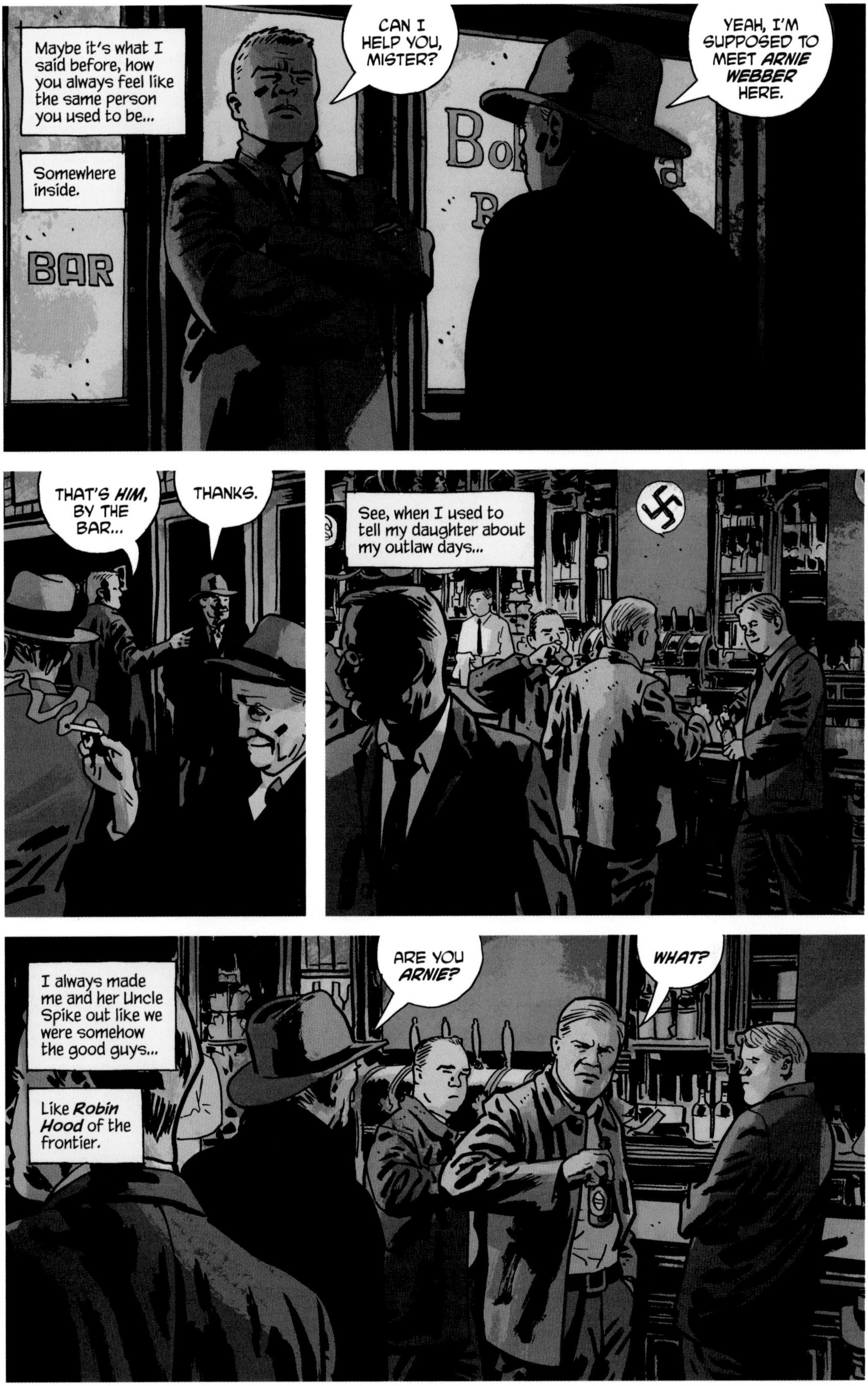
Maybe it's what I said before, how you always feel like the same person you used to be...
Somewhere inside.
BAR
CAN I HELP YOU, MISTER?
YEAH, I'M SUPPOSED TO MEET *ARNIE WEBBER* HERE.
THAT'S *HIM*, BY THE BAR...
THANKS.
See, when I used to tell my daughter about my outlaw days...
I always made me and her Uncle Spike out like we were somehow the good guys...
Like *Robin Hood* of the frontier.
ARE YOU *ARNIE?*
WHAT?

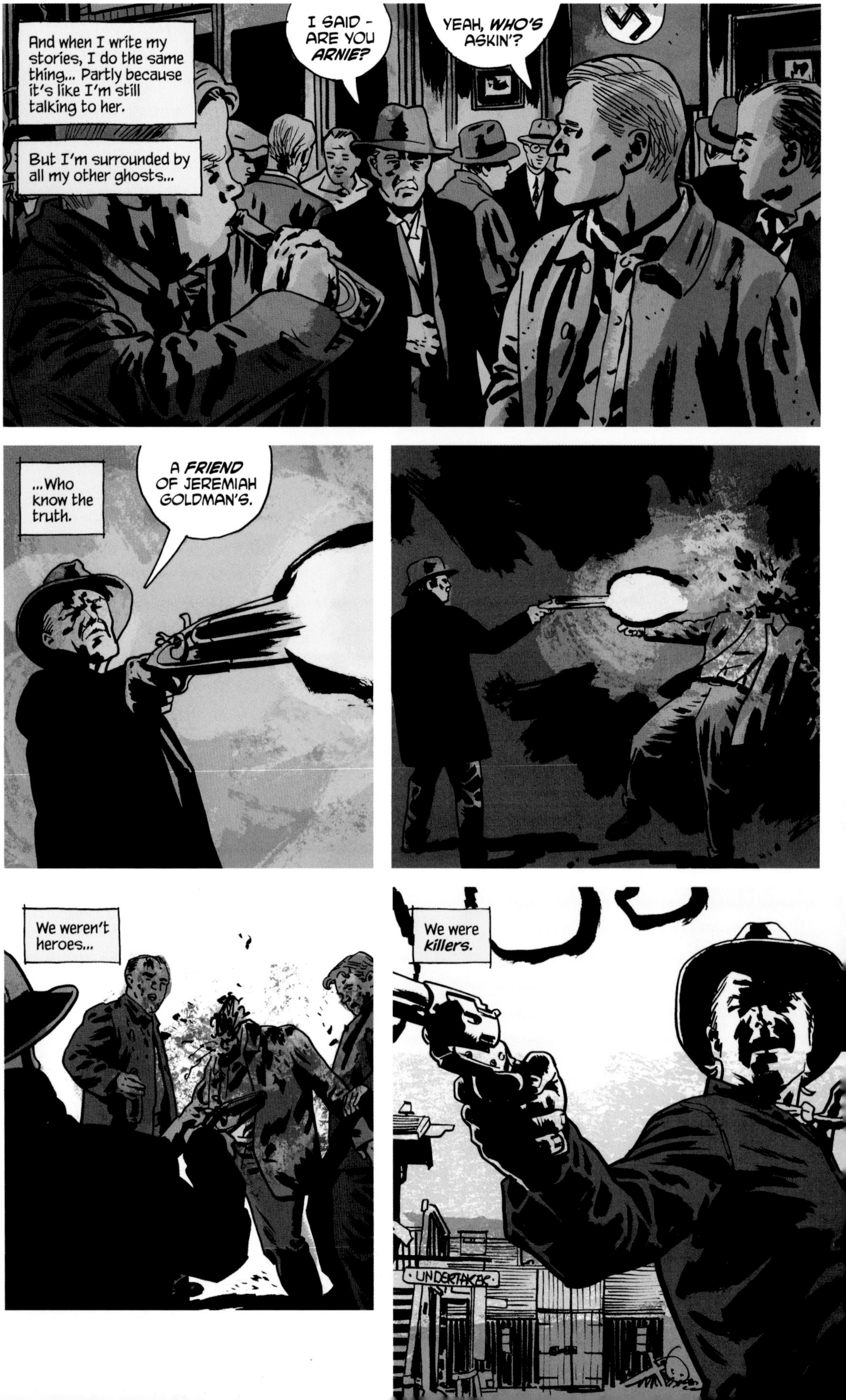
And when I write my stories, I do the same thing... Partly because it's like I'm still talking to her.
But I'm surrounded by all my other ghosts...
I SAID - ARE YOU *ARNIE?*
YEAH, *WHO'S* ASKIN'?
...Who know the truth.
A *FRIEND* OF JEREMIAH GOLDMAN'S.
We weren't heroes...
We were *killers.*
UNDERTAKER

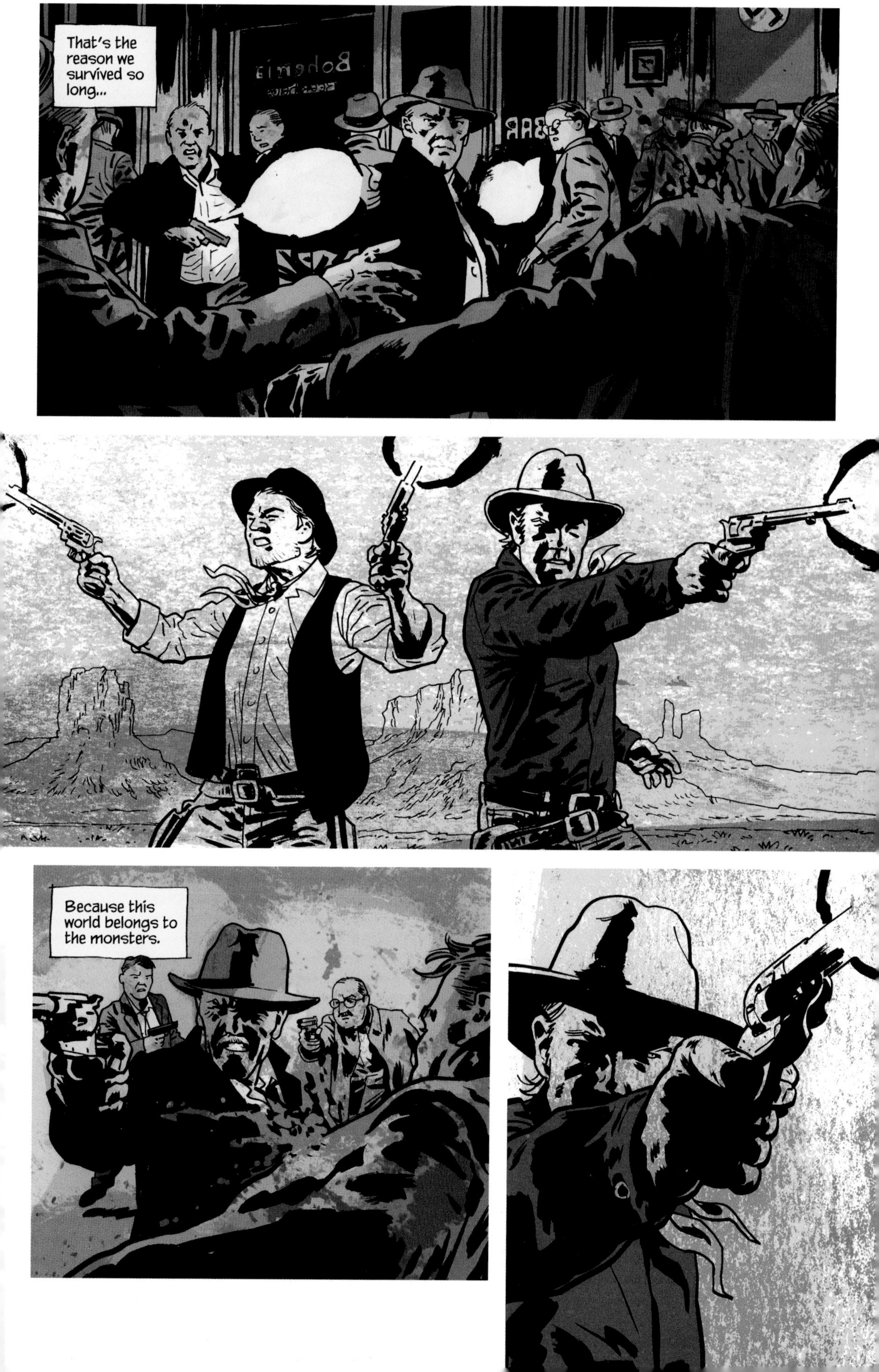
That's the reason we survived so long...
Because this world belongs to the monsters.

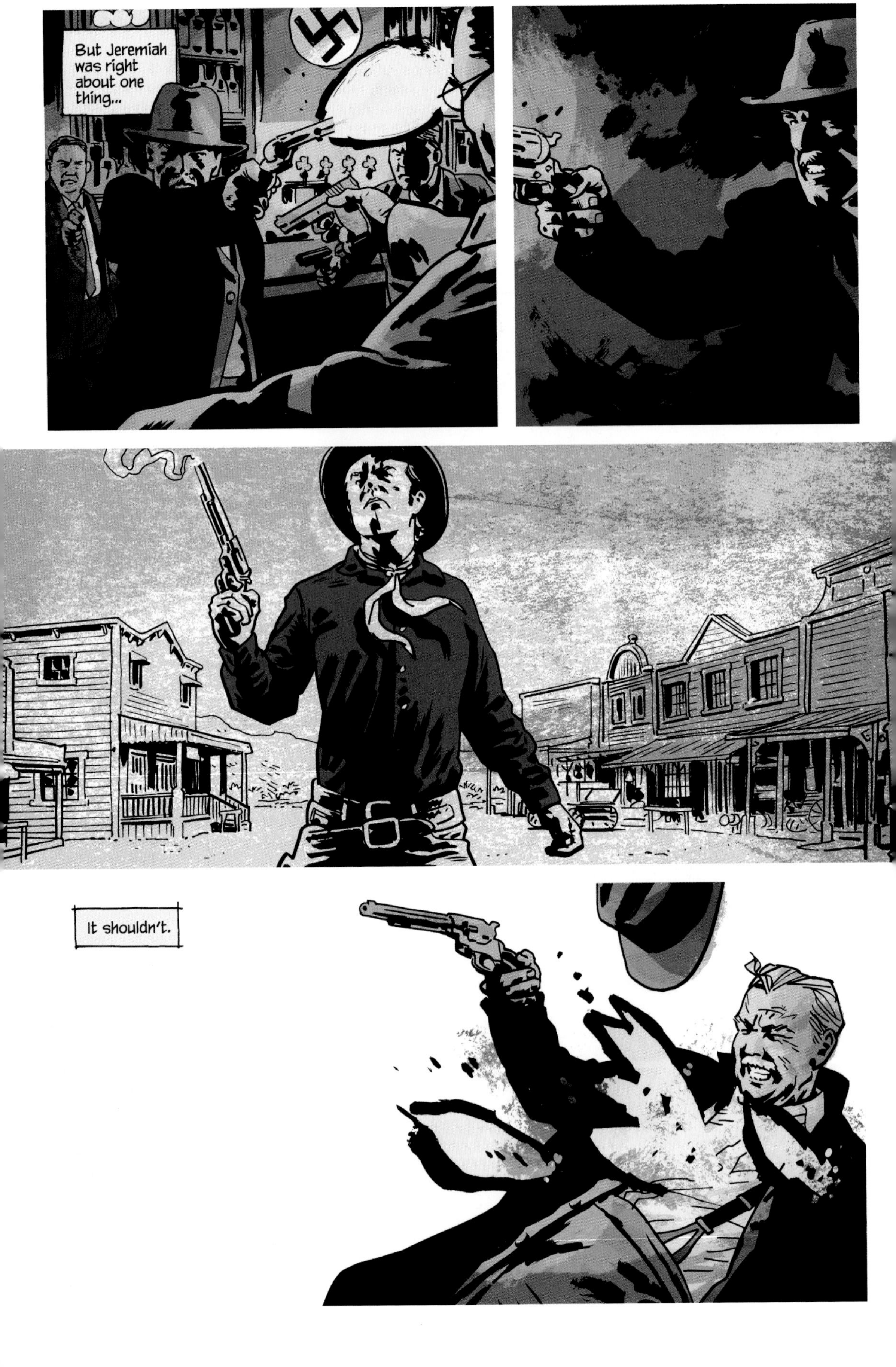
But Jeremiah was right about one thing...
It shouldn't.

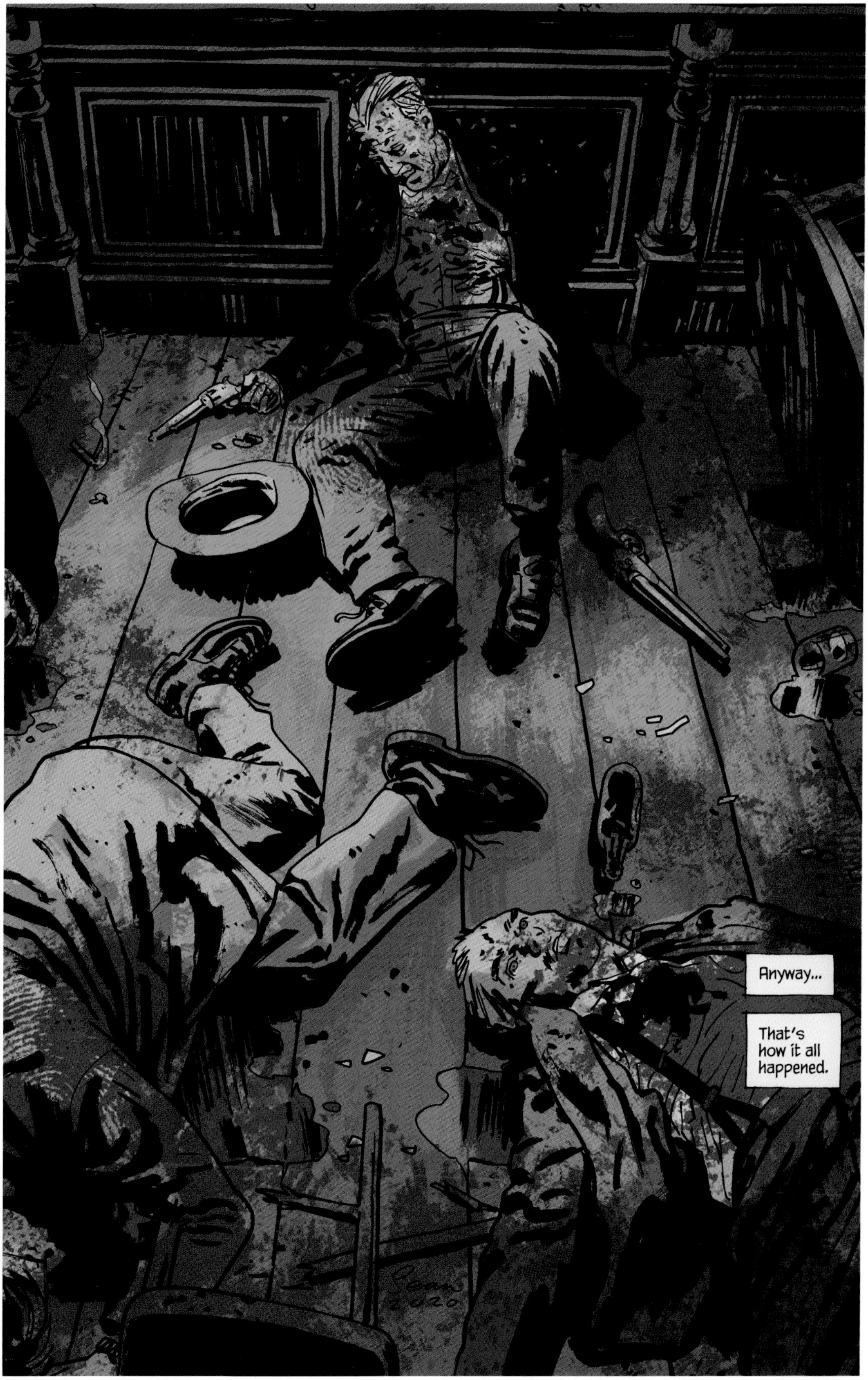
Anyway...
That's how it all happened.

For a book this research-heavy, it surprised me how often I was asked if there really was a Nazi rally in Madison Square Garden in February of 1939. But there was, and the protest outside did in fact draw a huge contingent of the NYPD to the front lines. It was an ugly night that Americans should never forget, and that sadly still feels relevant today, maybe moreso than ever.

Here's some of the actual press coverage of the night, from the NY Daily News, the NY Times, and the AP, and a still from the documentary A NIGHT AT THE GARDEN from Field of Vision.

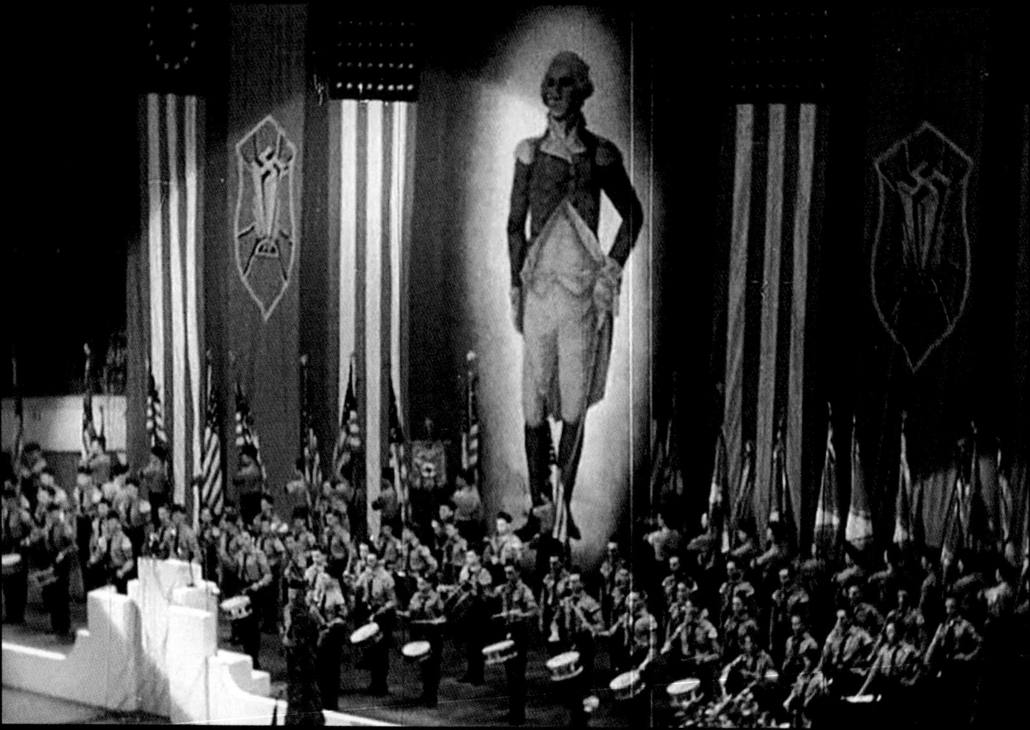

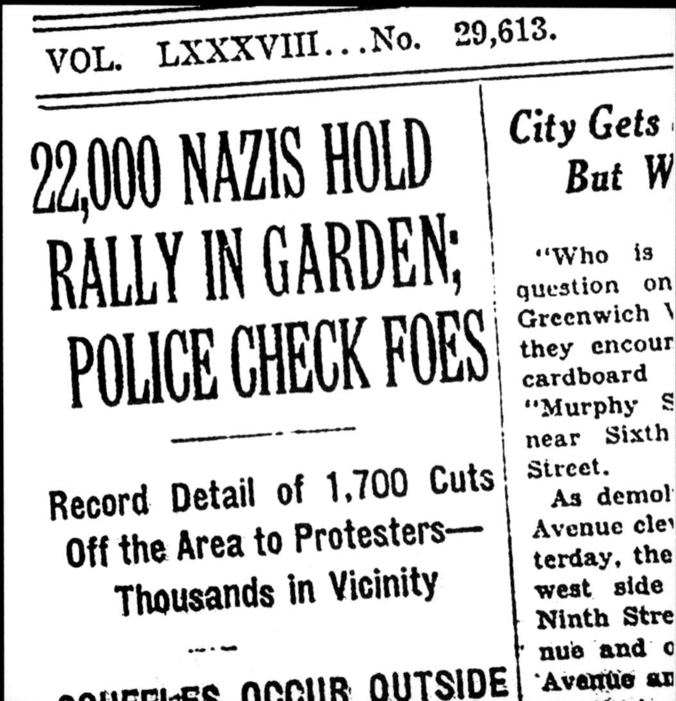

VOL. LXXXVIII...No. 29,613.

22,000 NAZIS HOLD RALLY IN GARDEN; POLICE CHECK FOES

Record Detail of 1,700 Cuts Off the Area to Protesters— Thousands in Vicinity

SCUFFLES OCCUR OUTSIDE

City Gets
But W

"Who is
question on
Greenwich
they encour
cardboard
"Murphy S
near Sixth
Street.
As demol
Avenue cle
terday, the
west side
Ninth Stre
nue and
Avenue an

Socialists Oppose Rally

WORKERS OF NEW YORK!

Stop the Fascists!

PICKET MADISON SQUARE GARDEN, MON., FEB. 20, 6 P.M.!

The fascists are mobilizing at Madison Square Garden Monday night.

Hitler's German-American Bund gangsters, Pelley's Silver Shirt scum and Coughlin's mob of labor-haters have hurled a brazen challenge at the workers of New York.

Wrapping themselves in the cloak of patriotism and "Americanism", the fascists prepare to spew their anti-labor and anti-Jewish poison throughout New York City.

These gangs have already gone too far. They must be stopped.

What are you going to do to stop this murderous crew?

We must not let this filthy, creeping slime get a foothold in New York. Gather in front of Madison Square Garden Monday by the thousands!

Be there at 6:00 P.M. sharp!

Let the fascists feel the anger and the might of the working class— Get out and picket!

Don't wait for the concentration camps—Act now!

On to Madison Square Garden Monday Night!

Issued by the
SOCIALIST WORKERS PARTY (Fourth International)
116 University Pla., New York City

This fiery Socialist circular was one of the reasons Police Commissioner Valentine will place strong police cordon around Madison Square Garden for German-American Bund rally tonight.

1,327 Cops Called Out to Guard Nazis In Rally at Garden

By ROBERT CONWAY.

The most drastic police precautions in recent years were taken yesterday following reports that three bombs would be planted inside Madison Square Garden, timed to explode during the German-American Bund rally there tonight.

A twenty-four hour guard of fifteen patrolmen and a sergeant was placed on duty immediately. Detectives of the bomb squad combed the interior of the Garden and Fire Department's Prevention bureau made a thorough inspection.

In all, 1,327 policemen have been assigned to the event—one of the largest police assignments in the city's history.

Further emergency orders were issued yesterday in preparation for the Nazi meeting, which is expected to bring into the area at least 60,000 Fascists and anti-Fascists, their tempers aroused by a week of ominous threats. But they

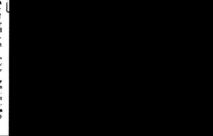

Wild Scenes In Madison Square Garden As Nazis Hold Rally

NEW YORK, Feb. 21. (AP) — In a Nazi demonstration that filled vast Madison Square Garden, leaders of the German-American Bund stood last night under the sign of the Swastika to denounce "international Jewry," some members of the Roosevelt cabinet, and any American alliance with European democracies.

While uniformed troopers marched intermittently inside the garden —which at official estimate held 20,000—a moving throng of anti-Nazis, theatregoers and the merely curious, milled about in the streets outside.

About 1,500 police reserves stood guard over the area, while violence spurted up inside the garden and out.

As Fritz Kuhn, national leader of the Bund, was concluding a peroration against Jews, Isadore Greenbaum, a slight, 26-year-old hotel worker, leaped upon the great stage and ran toward the speaker.

Instantly, a dozen or more storm troopers set upon him, knocking him down and beating him as he held his head in his arms, his black, wild hair flying.

A squad of police pushed the storm troopers aside, picked him from the floor of the platform and, holding him high above their heads, ran to an exit. Most of his clothing was torn from his body.

Later, he was booked for disorderly conduct and held in $100 bail.

Outside the garden, 13 persons altogether were arrested in a series of fights involving the police — who refused permission of anti-Nazis to picket the garden—and the followers and opponents of Nazism.

The first disturbance at the meeting involved Dorothy Thompson, newspaper columnist, who had shouted "nonsense" during a speech by G. W. Kunze, the bund's national publicity director.

Amid shouts of "sit down" and "throw her out," a grey-shirted storm trooper and two policemen started to hustle her from the building. Heywood Broun, another columnist, ran to her rescue, telling the police her identity. She was allowed to remain upon her insistence that "American free speech" gave her the right to express disagreement with any speaker.

The most extraordinary police (Continued on Page 2)

For More From Brubaker and Phillips

Ed Brubaker
Sean Phillips
CRIMINAL
Coward

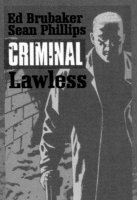

Ed Brubaker
Sean Phillips
CRIMINAL
Lawless

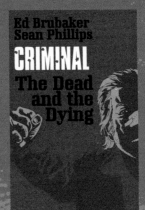

Ed Brubaker
Sean Phillips
CRIMINAL
The Dead and the Dying

Ed Brubaker
Sean Phillips
CRIMINAL
Bad Night

ED BRUBAKER SEAN PHILLIPS
FATALE
BOOK ONE
DEATH CHASES ME

ED BRUBAKER SEAN PHILLIPS
FATALE
BOOK TWO
THE DEVIL'S BUSINESS

ED BRUBAKER SEAN PHILLIPS
FATALE
BOOK THREE
WEST OF HELL

ED BRUBAKER SEAN PHILLIPS
FATALE
BOOK FOUR
PRAY FOR RAIN

Volume One
KILL or be KILLED
Ed Brubaker
Sean Phillips
Elizabeth Breitweiser

Volume Two
KILL or be KILLED
Ed Brubaker
Sean Phillips
Elizabeth Breitweiser

Volume Three
KILL or be KILLED
Ed Brubaker
Sean Phillips
Elizabeth Breitweiser

Volume Four
KILL or be KILLED
Ed Brubaker
Sean Phillips
Elizabeth Breitweiser

"One of the best graphic novels of the year." - GQ
The FADE OUT
Ed BRUBAKER Sean PHILLIPS

"One of comics dream teams delivers their best story yet in THE FADE OUT, an old Hollywood murder mystery draped against HUAC and the Red Scare."

– New York Magazine

Ed Brubaker
Sean Phillips
CRIMINAL
The Sinners

Ed Brubaker
Sean Phillips
CRIMINAL
The Last of the Innocent

Ed Brubaker
Sean Phillips
CRIMINAL
Wrong Time Wrong Place

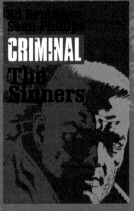

"CRIMINAL is equal parts John Woo's THE KILLER, Stanley Kubrick's THE KILLING, and Francis Ford Coppola's THE GODFATHER."

– Playboy Magazine

ED BRUBAKER SEAN PHILLIPS
FATALE
BOOK FIVE
CURSE THE DEMON

ED BRUBAKER SEAN PHILLIPS
FATALE
THE DELUXE EDITION VOLUME ONE

ED BRUBAKER SEAN PHILLIPS
FATALE
THE DELUXE EDITION VOLUME TWO

"Immortality may be a double-edged sword, but it's one the intoxicating Jo wields with a boundless grace in this addictive page-turner."

– Publishers Weekly

Ed Brubaker
Sean Phillips
KILL or be KILLED
THE DELUXE EDITION

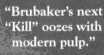

"Brubaker's next "Kill" oozes with modern pulp."

– USAToday

"KILL OR BE KILLED is magnificent, a true thing of beauty in a tale that is so damn ugly."

– Nerdist

Ed Brubaker
Sean Phillips
CRIMINAL
UNDERTOW
The Deluxe Edition Volume One

Ed Brubaker
Sean Phillips
CRIMINAL
The Deluxe Edition Volume Two

Ed Brubaker
Sean Phillips
CRIMINAL
The Deluxe Edition Volume Three

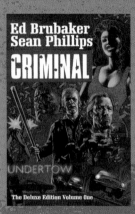

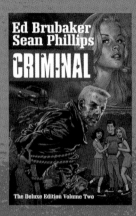

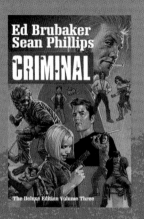

"Sean Phillips and Ed Brubaker represent the gold standard for comics noir - brutal, beautiful and best."

– Ian Rankin, author of the John Rebus novels

"The powerhouse creative team of Brubaker and Phillips combine elements of noir and coming-of-age stories in this psychologically and emotionally complex drama about desperate men and women daring to strive for better lives in a violent world where hope and love are dangerous liabilities."

– Library Journal

CRUEL
SUMMER
Ed Brubaker
Sean Phillips

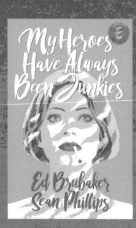

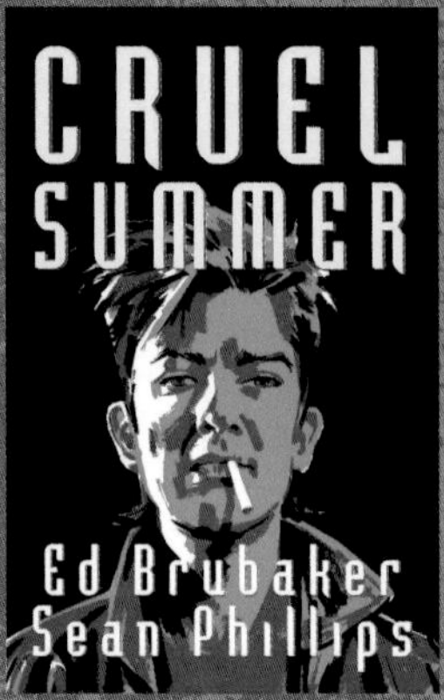

Newsweek's Best Comic Books of 2018

Thrillist's Best Comics & Graphic Novels

Diamond Gem Award for Best Original Graphic novel 2018

My Heroes Have Always Been Junkies
Ed Brubaker
Sean Phillips

Eisner Award Winner – Best Original Graphic Novel

Ringo Award Winner – Best Original Graphic Novel

"Far and away the best work yet from one of the best teams in the history of comics."

– Brian K. Vaughan (PAPER GIRLS, SAGA)

Bad
Weekend
Ed Brubaker
Sean Phillips

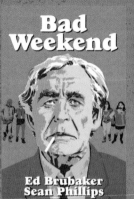

"Easily one of the best comics of the 21st century... a story that reflects the crooked soul of our times."

– Tom King (Mr Miracle, Sheriff of Babylon)

ED BRUBAKER
SEAN PHILLIPS
PULP

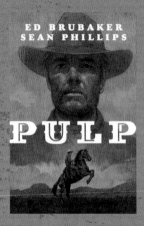

"Oh man this book pushed EVERY crime fiction button for me. Bliss."

– Patton Oswalt

"I love this book."

Damon Lindelof – LOST, HBO's Watchmen

"RECKLESS is an absolute rush. You gotta have it."

– Joe Hill (Locke & Key, N0S4A2)

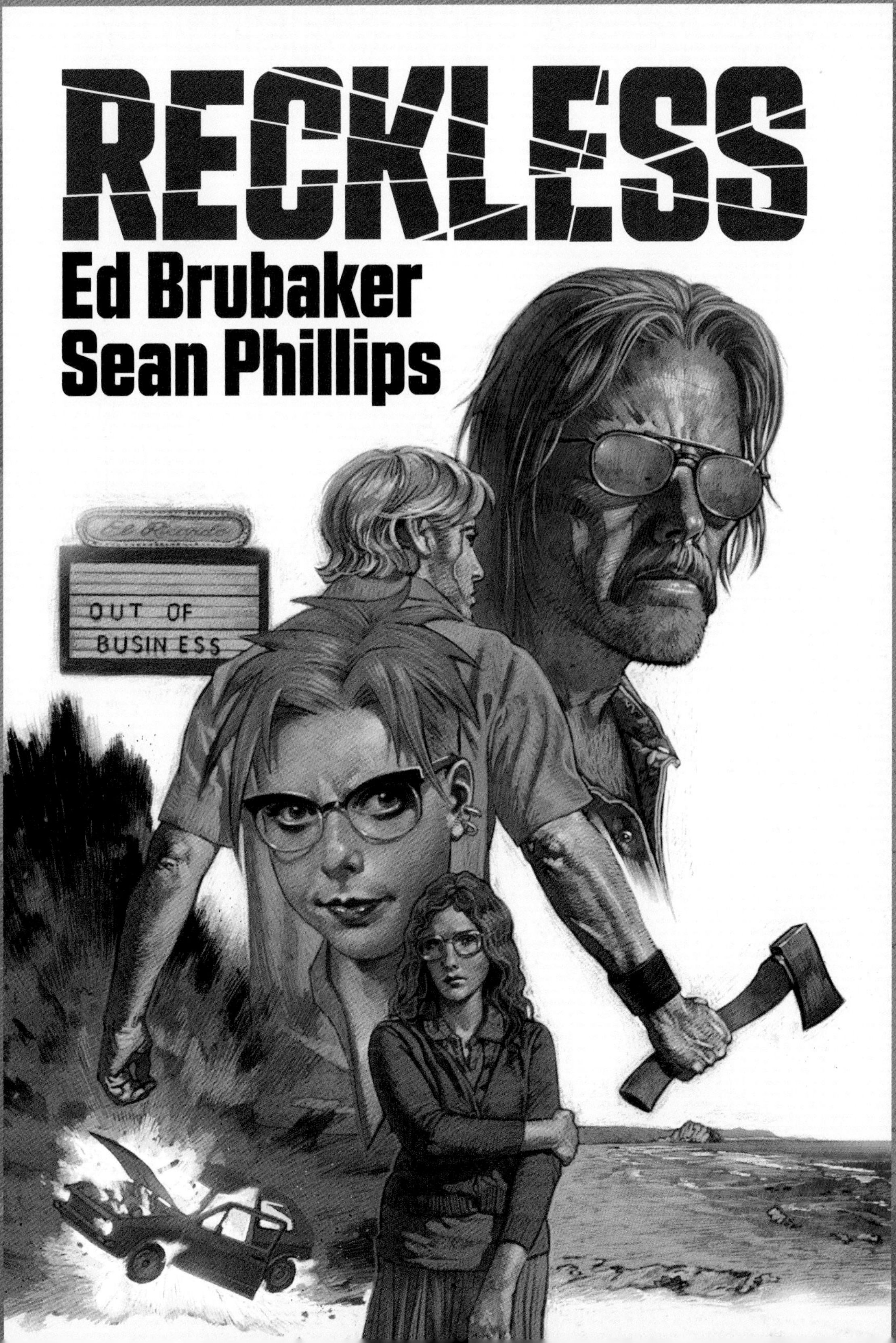
RECKLESS
Ed Brubaker
Sean Phillips
OUT OF
BUSIN ESS

Biographies

Ed Brubaker is one of the most acclaimed writers in comics, having won the Eisner and Harvey Awards for Best Writer five times, among others. His many graphic novels with artist Sean Phillips have been published around the world in several languages. Moving into television writing, Brubaker first served as a Supervising Producer on HBO's WESTWORLD, and then with director Nicolas Winding Refn, he was co-creator and writer of Amazon's TOO OLD TO DIE YOUNG, the first streaming series to debut at Cannes.

Brubaker lives with his wife and dog in California, where he continues to work in film, television, and as always, comics.

Drawing comics professionally since the age of fifteen, Eisner Award-winning Sean Phillips has worked for all the major publishers. Since drawing Sleeper, Hellblazer, Batman, X-Men, Marvel Zombies, and Stephen King's The Dark Tower, Sean has concentrated on creator-owned books including CRIMINAL, KILL OR BE KILLED, INCOGNITO, FATALE and THE FADE OUT.

He is currently drawing the second in a new series of graphic novels written by his long-time collaborator Ed Brubaker and coloured by his son Jacob Phillips.

He lives in the Lake District in the UK.

Jacob Phillips is a freelance illustrator based in Manchester, England. When he was just 11 years old he wrote, drew and home-printed his first comic book, Roboy. He took this to Brighton Comic Convention and sold it from behind a table, selling out on the first day. Ever since, he has been scribbling away, working with clients such as the BBC, Arrow Film, Headspace Property, Arte and Kino Lorber.

Jacob is the current colorist on Ed Brubaker and Sean Phillips' CRIMINAL as well as working as a freelance illustrator and comic book artist. He has recently completed work on his first comic as a solo artist, THAT TEXAS BLOOD, with writer Chris Condon and is currently working on a new Image title with a top-secret Eisner Award-winning writer.